Sinners & Other Saints

Nancy Crouchman

2013
© Nancy Crouchman

ISBN 978-1-927265-00-0   (paperback)
ISBN 978-1-927265-01-7   (ePub)
ISBN 978-1-927265-02-4   (Mobi)

PO BOX 4075 MOUNT MAUNGANUI SOUTH
BAY OF PLENTY 3149 NEW ZEALAND-AOTEAROA
http://www.oceanbooks.co.nz

Contents

Sinners & Other Saints

Special thanks to my husband Glenn, Jenny Argante and Mike Dunwoody for making this collection possible.

Push

Glenn Miller speaks to me from our living room. 'Chattanooga Choo Choo' blasts out from the radio. His lyrics inspire me:

"Step aside partner, it's my day. I've got my fare and just a trifle to spare."

Well, I've got my savings too, and I've made up my mind. This time I'm going to the hospital to have our fifth. No more home births for this forty-year-old. I'm going to get on board and enjoy the ride.

In nine months my meager savings have grown from spare change to a healthy roll of dollar bills. I've been squirreling away part of the rent from my two tenants, and I'm careful to save every penny, buying day-old bread, dented cans of fruit and vegetables and thrift-shop clothes for myself and the kids.

My penny-pinching adds up to just enough to cover the cost for a week's stay in the hospital. Doc thinks my idea is a good one. He did say, "These change of life babies can be tricky."

Now it's my one chance to do something nice for myself and this baby.

July has to be the worst month to give birth in Windsor. The Ontario humidity and mosquitoes are driving me crazy, but my due date is coming up fast and my hopes are in high gear.

Six years is a long time between babies, but I should have lots of help from the older kids.

My husband Joe works long hours at his auto parts shop next door and is usually too tired to be of much help. This doesn't bother me as I just want him to stay off the booze and be there for me and the kids. It's been three months since his last binge and customary sincere apology.

"I know I've let you down, Ada, but now that we're having another baby I promise this time I will join AA and get off the booze for good."

Joe loves babies, especially his own. He can hardly wait. I think he's even more excited than I am.

As for myself, I spend a lot of time writing letters to the editor of the local newspaper under my alias 'Pug.' It's no surprise to my friends because they all call me Pug. I think my nickname probably started because I have a rather cute pug nose. Or could it be short for 'pugnacious'?

I know I like to bitch about our corrupt police department and the Italians who operate 'Blind Pigs' in our neighbourhood, but that's about all I can do. Seeing my words in print gives me a real high. I keep a scrapbook with all my published letters. Sometimes I even fantasize that some day one of my kids will be smart enough and free enough to write books just like a real writer.

The contractions started this morning, and now they're a half-hour apart. It's time for me to get a move on. When I walk next door to ask Joe to drive me to the hospital I can't see him in the shop or anywhere in the yard. I ask the young man working behind the counter.

"Have you seen Joe around? We've got to get to the hospital."

"Sorry, Ada, but he left for the day."

"What do you mean, he left? You mean he took off again? That bastard!"

Choking back tears, I go home to pick up my packed bag with my new nightgown, underwear and a pretty dress I made and to get my stash from a mason jar hidden in the kitchen cupboard. It's a good thing we live just a half-block away from the bus-stop. I'm so nervous that at first I can't find my jar. It's been moved to the back of a higher shelf. *I hope I don't fall off this damn kitchen chair.*

No! This can't be true!

All my dollar bills that were tied together with elastic bands are gone! Only a few coins are left.

You've turned my life upside down again. I hate you, Joe.

War is waging in Europe and now my own battle is soon to erupt. But right now I must be strong and have this baby at home.

At times like this I'm grateful to have a teenage daughter to take my youngest to the park for the day, and an unemployed roomer to call the doctor. I hear myself yell out orders like a drill-sergeant.

"Tell him to come over right away. I'll be in bed. Betty, keep a close eye on Ann.

Remember she's only six. Joey, go look for your dad and tell him he better get home."

I lie in the middle of our sagging double mattress and stare at the crumbling plaster ceiling.

Cobwebs are laughing at me dressed in my tent-like, threadbare nightgown. I don't want to get blood on my new one. I'll get to those dusty streamers when this party is over. It's lucky I washed the sheets yesterday; maybe I'm psychic.

Joe is probably drinking red wine somewhere in this heat. I sure hope he's wearing a cap. The kids will be home soon. I don't want them to come into the bedroom. What'll we have for supper? Relax. Breathe. Focus on white clouds.

I remember our first six years of marriage before Virgil was born, before the drinking started. Our honeymoon at Niagara-on-the-Lake with quiet walks on the beach, Joe's handmade fruit basket filled with our picnic lunch. Breathe. Focus. Laughing on a swing. Push me higher, Joe… Higher…I want to touch the sky.

Now I can hear another man's voice say, "Push, push. Harder… harder. You're almost there."

I feel the rough texture of a bleached flour sack against my cheek. It's pretending to be a pillow case, but I know 'Five Roses Flour' is printed smack in the middle of my floral embroidery.

Get a grip, Ada… After all, Mom had eleven kids and she didn't go to the hospital! Stop whining. Stop feeling sorry for yourself. This suffering is nothing in comparison to what may be in store for me.

Why did I agree to give up my secretarial job when we got married? Maybe Joe's ego couldn't accept a woman making her own money. He only has a Grade Three education, but he's a hard worker and he's smart. I know my family felt I could have done better. I remember Mom telling me, "If you burn your ass you have to sit on the blisters."

Joe, is that you? Where the hell are you? It hurts, it really hurts… Damn you. Did you forget me? Why aren't you here? You know I need you. I can't take this pain. Help me… I love you, Joe.

Billie Holliday's words 'God Bless the Child' are playing in my head.

> *"Them that's got shall get*
> *Them that's got shall lose*
> *So the Bible said and it still is news*
> *Mama may have, Papa may have*
> *But God bless the child that's got his own*
> *That's got his own."*

Dr. Sanborn urges me along, "Come on, Ada. Push. You can do it."

This kid is going to be different… I know it's the beginning of something special and wonderful.

I hear the doctor say, "Congratulations, Ada. She's perfect. I bet she'll have beautiful big blue eyes just like you."

As my scrawny baby girl comes wriggling out into this cruel, cold world I silently pray for her, this little Nancy Marilyn, to *really* push herself to make more of her life than I did. I know it's too late for me.

My train has left the station. I'm stuck.

Sins of my Father

1.   Acts of Contrition

I knew I had the best dad in the world. I was the baby of the family and my sisters and brothers said he spoiled me rotten. But they were just as guilty. Candy, popsicles, pop and anything else I wanted was always available. I was learning that they all wanted life to be better for me than it had been for them.

Much of my formal education began long before I went to Grade One in 1947. Even as a toddler, Dad often took me to work with him at his auto parts shop next door.   I didn't talk much, but I did love to listen to the guys when they said they were 'just shooting the shit.'

After work I practiced reciting that day's new vocabulary. 'Kiss my ass' and 'Bugger off' were two of my favourites.   My brothers Pete and Joey laughed their heads off, but I never got so much as a smile from Mom or my sisters Betty and Ann.

Looking for some discipline Mom told Dad I had called the bank manager a 'son of a bitch' while she was making a deposit.   Dad just shook his head and said with a smile, "You're right, kiddo; he really is a son of a bitch. I can't punish you for telling the truth."

It was fun being with my family. Often it felt like we were having a party, but not always. Dad played his mouth organ and made the clicking of two teaspoons sound like music while he danced his famous jig. Sometimes he challenged his friends and my brothers to 'pull arms' at the kitchen table. When he won the match he took out his false teeth and waved them in the air like a trophy.

Dad got into a lot of fights when he was drunk. Everyone knew he was proud to be nicknamed 'Tojo.' His black, round spectacles made him look just like the fierce Japanese warrior. He also thought it was funny when he pretended to be a real tough guy and yelled 'Heil Hitler' while he stood at attention and saluted with one arm stretched out. He bragged about being able to beat up all the guys at the bar, even if they were twice his size. Pete and Joey must have been proud of Dad because they wanted to learn how to fight and get drunk just like him.

I remember when I was about four or five years-old Dad often disappeared for a week or so. When he finally came home he always gave Mom a present and repeated his usual apology.

"Sorry, Ada. I swear I won't take off again. I promise. Here, these are for you."

Seeing the picture of the pretty lady on the white box in the gold and black cameo I knew it was Laura Secord. We all agreed that she made the best chocolates we had ever tasted. I wondered why Mom looked so sad when she handed us the unopened box without even taking one for herself. Maybe she was tired from doing so much cooking and canning, as well as all the cleaning and laundry for our roomers. But we were thrilled; more chocolates for the rest of us.

My hopes for the best holiday ever went down the drain one Christmas Eve when we heard a loud crash in the basement. Ann held my hand as we crept down the stairs behind Mom. We saw all her precious canned peaches, plums and tomatoes swimming in broken glass and syrup. Dad stood there stunned by the disgusting sight, holding a bottle of wine he had pulled from its hiding place behind the now-collapsed shelf of preserves.

With tears in his eyes Dad staggered up the stairs as he pleaded, "I'm sorry, Ada. It was an accident. I promise I'm going to get sober for good."

Mom kept silent as she continued to wring her hands.

Ann whispered, "Don't cry, Mom, I'll help you clean up this mess."

When Dad stumbled into the living room and fell into our Christmas tree, Mom heaved it out onto our snow-covered front yard as she yelled, "Go to bed and sleep it off, Joe. You've done enough damage for one day."

Homemade ornaments, red bulbs and icicles decorated our entrance until New Year's Day. Now I understand why Mom always said, "Christmas is just another day."

Going to AA meetings was a special treat for me. After the speeches were over I got to eat huge sugar cookies and brownies with chocolate icing on top. On the way home from the backseat of our car I listened to Dad make lots of promises and big plans. It all sounded so good. Their voices were low and happy. We believed him once more.

Before long their bedroom smelled of vomit again. Even with the window open it didn't blow away the foul odor or Mom's sadness. But worse than the stink was the sound of his screams. I overheard Mom say to her friend, "Joe's been at it again. He has the DTs and the shakes."

Later I found out what she meant. No wonder he cried out when he saw snakes and rats crawling up the wall. Who wouldn't?

Dad wasn't the same person when he tried to sober up, nothing at all like the Dad I knew. He didn't want to dance or pull arms. He sat and watched wrestling on TV. Maybe I liked him better when he was drunk.

He left us again, but this time it would be for more than a week. Mom lied to the neighbours in her brightest voice when she said he was off working on the boats. But the truth about his conviction for possession of stolen goods made headlines in the *Windsor Star*. Her secret was out. She would have to buck-up and learn to swallow her pride and carry on without him.

With a big hug she tried to comfort me by saying, "Don't worry, Nancy. He'll be out of jail and back home in a couple of years."

Sins of my Father

2.   Penance

It was my first road trip and I could hardly wait to go to Guelph. My brother Joey hoisted me up as he exclaimed, "We're going to visit Dad in the hoosegow."

Rather than saying reformatory or jail our family liked to say 'hoosegow'. Somehow this silly name sounded better.

Mom was almost giddy as she hummed some unknown tune while she packed peanut butter and jam sandwiches, and some yummy oatmeal cookies.

"It'll be fun," she said. We can have a picnic on the way."

Joey had polished Dad's filthy '37 Hudson so we could hardly recognize it, and he had also checked the oil and inspected the tires. I think he felt proud to be the man of the house now that his older brother had joined the Air Force.

I remember begging Mom, "Please let me wear my First Communion dress so Dad can see how pretty I looked on my big day."

At last she agreed. But when I wanted to wear my veil and carry my prayer book she whispered in her gentle voice, "Don't be silly, Nancy. We aren't going to church."

It felt like the three-hour drive took forever, even though we were going fast at fifty miles an hour. I kept bugging Joey with my constant whining.

"Are we there yet?"

He joked, "Button up kid, or you can walk the rest of the way."

Mom consoled me.

"It'll be faster going home. You're excited now, and that always makes the time go by slowly. Let's play I Spy and before you know it, we'll be there."

Dad had been behind bars for six months for buying and selling stolen auto parts, and I really missed him. No one else seemed interested in playing house with me. His letters were hard to read after the guards blacked out some of his words. Mom held the letter up to the light, but that didn't help. She knew his language was probably rude and loaded with cuss words about the guards.

She reminded us once again.

"Everyone knows your dad can't say one sentence without swearing, but he doesn't deserve to be behind bars. He never stole a thing in his life".

At long last we finally arrived. I wished we had a Kodak to take some pictures. The prison looked like a mansion built out of rocks, like something in the movies. It was so beautiful. I believed Dad was really lucky to live in this palace.

I couldn't see any swings, monkey-bars or slides in the park around the enormous building. The grass seemed to be laid out like a soft, green carpet. It would be perfect for me and my friends to roll around on. We noticed two flags mounted on either side of the huge entrance doors, their wings proudly flying.

Joey piped in, "They're Union Jacks."

I thought that was a silly name to call flags! My uncle Jack is a man, and my friend has a dog called Jack, but I had never heard of a Union Jack.

Mom and I held hands as we walked up the stairs to the front entrance. Joey, like a gentleman, opened the heavy door for us. Two tall men in dark blue uniforms asked Mom to sign all our names in a large book lying on a long desk.

After they looked inside Mom's purse and checked our pockets, we were escorted into a big room filled with tables and chairs. These men were short on words and shorter on smiles. Instead of calling my mother Mrs Yager, they called her Ma'am. They didn't call me or my brother anything, as if we weren't there.

"There's Dad!"

I spotted him right away coming towards us. He looked like I remembered him, only a little thinner, and his face seemed pale. He lifted me up as he gave me a big hug and kiss. Then he complimented me in a loud voice so everyone could hear, "Damn it, Nancy, you look lovely, just like an angel. Your dress is beautiful. You must have been the prettiest girl in the church."

Mom got a huge bear- hug and a kiss on the lips. After playfully slapping Joey on the back he asked him, "So how's life on the outside? Do you miss your old man?"

"It's okay, but what about you? We all wish you were home."

"I'm fine. I just have to mind my own business and keep my nose clean. They got me working in the carpentry shop. I sure like the feel of making something nice out of wood. It beats the hell out of buying and selling auto parts, especially the hot stuff that got me in here."

Dad rubbed his eyes with his knuckles before he continued. "Now, Ada, what about our roomers, are they paying their rent?"

She rhymed off their nicknames. "Pickles, Red Cross, and Duke the stuffed shirt. They're all paid right up to date, but I might have to use the padlock on the new guy. He's already behind by two weeks."

"That son of a bitch! Do whatever it takes to collect the cash, even if it means locking the bastard out." He softened his voice when he said, "When the joker pays, treat yourself to a perm at the Beauty School. It's been a long time since we had any extra money, and God knows you deserve it."

After a while a harsh voice came over the loud-speaker.

"Time's up.

Visitors' hours are now over."

I gave Dad a quick kiss and said, "Don't forget to write me lots of letters."

Mom wiped away some tears as she hugged him. Joey, head down, bolted out the door without saying goodbye.

On the way home I couldn't help thinking that we came all that way for a half-hour visit. It wasn't worth it. I didn't even get to look at anything inside the postcard-perfect building, and I didn't see Dad's cell. Next time I'd rather stay home, and play house with my friends.

We never did go back, but Mom and I wrote to him faithfully every week. My letters were always the same.

Dear Dad,
I love you.
Do you love me?
Yes or no?
Love, Nancy xxxx

Sins of my Father

3. Absolution

*"...forgive us our trespasses
as we forgive those who trespass against
us..."*

Time to bury him. Dad had fifty-seven years under his belt and now we had to let him go. AA couldn't cure his cirrhosis of the liver, and a massive heart attack caught our undaunted hero off guard. He should have seen it coming. We all should have seen it coming.

The shrill ring came at two in the morning as I lay huddled next to Mom in their double bed. Sixteen was too old to sleep with my mother, but we needed to be close to each other since the day the ambulance took him away.

We rushed into the kitchen to answer the phone. Mom held it between us as we strained to hear the lady's voice.

"I'm sorry, Mrs Yager. Your husband has passed away. He went quickly without pain. You're welcome to visit him to say your final goodbye before his body is removed."

He had survived for two nights breathing with the aid of an oxygen tank; unable to communicate, eat or drink. I had my chance to say goodbye that day at the hospital, to tell Dad how much I loved him. Instead I watched from the hallway through the open door of his room as life oozed from his limp, ashen body.

He had done this to himself and now we were going to pay the price. Who would look after us? We didn't want him to go.

Thoughts came back in bits and flashbacks at unsuspecting moments. The first day Dad attempted to teach me how to drive, I heard his panicked voice yell, "Jesus, Nancy, do you want to give me a goddam heart attack?"

That afternoon when he climbed out of the passenger side of his 1950 Ford was my last driving lesson with Dad. He quit on the spot. Instead he conscripted my brother Joey to risk his life with me until I finally got my license. That was a year before he died.

I refused to believe that Dad was really gone. Surely he would come back carrying his usual box of chocolates. I willed myself to think he was playing some kind of trick, or that he was off on another binge. Soon we would see his feet stomping on the linoleum floor, and listen to the clicking sound of spoons as he danced his familiar jig.

Mom made all of the arrangements for the funeral. She was probably thinking that the love of her life would be so proud to be laid out in such a fine piece of furniture, dressed in his only suit and black bow tie. The coffin cost more than she could afford, but she wanted to give him a royal send off.

Being a carpenter, he would surely appreciate the quality of solid walnut. Mom brought him his expensive Dack shoes so he could go out in style. Our condescending neighbours didn't see the always polished, size 10 black wingtips, but she knew he had them on. There was no way she wanted him buried in bare feet like a common beggar.

Approaching the open casket I pretended to look at the body. I knew someone was inside that wooden box, someone wearing Dad's clothes, but my real dad wasn't there.

My mind couldn't or wouldn't give up on him. I pleaded with him not to abandon us and give our family another chance. *Don't leave us alone, we need you. I forgive you. Mom forgives you. Please come back home. We're waiting for you.*

Black and White

By the time I turned eleven I was addicted. It was easy for me to get my TV fix at lunch-time because I could walk home from school in under ten minutes with enough time to eat and watch Search for Tomorrow, and still get back to school before the bell rang.

We lived in the inner city of Windsor and were the first family on our block to get a brand new 10-inch General Electric black and white TV. After school and weekends I sat glued to the set watching anything, but especially The Auntie Dee Show.

I was infatuated with this popular kids' talent contest program and dreamed of becoming a sensational star.

One Friday afternoon Mom greeted me from the kitchen.

"So how was school today, Nancy?"

"Same as every day. Nothing ever changes."

"You got a letter in the mail. Were you expecting something from a TV station?"

"No, I wasn't, but where is it?"

"Over there on the coffee table."

Oh, my God, please let it be a miracle.

After a long few seconds I grabbed the white legal size envelope and casually strolled off to my bedroom as my heart pounded wildly. Sure enough, it was addressed to me. Holding my breath, I sat on my unmade bed and ripped it open.

"Your application to audition for the Auntie Dee Talent Search Contest has been accepted. Please bring your sheet music for the song you intend to perform. Auditions will be held on Saturday November 7th 1952 at 10am. The WXYZ-TV Studio is located at 5057 Woodward Avenue in downtown Detroit."

I had taken voice lessons from the Ursuline nuns, but Beautiful Dreamer was not my idea of great music and besides the convent setting with all the penguin-like creatures parading down the long corridors gave me the creeps. I often wondered if they had any hair or dandruff under those black veils.

My voice didn't seem to be getting any better after three classes, so I threatened to quit. When the nuns didn't encourage me to continue, I dropped out just to teach them a lesson.

The Auntie Dee show was the number one children's talent search in the 1950s. An appearance on this program guaranteed exposure to a national audience.

I imagined signing autographs, and having guys go crazy over me. That's when I had decided to apply for an audition. I carefully typed my letter. My application should look like it was written by a real secretary, so after three hours on the old Underwood typewriter, and lots of corrections, I was satisfied with my efforts.

I mailed my entry, but in case I was rejected I had decided to keep my desire a secret. No one knew, not even my best friend Lucille, that I had sent in a request to appear on the show. I prayed I would be lucky and get my big break to become the next Canadian superstar.

Armed with overflowing enthusiasm I blurted out the news at the supper table.

"I'm going on the Auntie Dee show!"

Mom's face turned white as she said, "What do you mean?"

"That's what was in the letter. I've got to audition next week to get on the show."

No one seemed to be the least bit thrilled. In fact, the rest of my family went silent. They looked worried and a little glum. I thought they must be jealous since they didn't have any musical talent.

It was as though they became deaf and dumb when I spoke of my future career in showbiz. It was downright rude and ignorant when they kept trying to change the subject. I decided to forge ahead without their support.

After supper I rushed over to tell Lucille my news. As always she was thrilled to see her one and only white girlfriend. Her grand piano smile with her dazzling white teeth could have been used in a Colgate commercial.

"Guess what, Lucille? You won't believe this, but I got an audition to sing on the Auntie Dee show."

She looked stunned and appeared confused.

"You got to be joking."

"No, I'm not kidding. This is my big chance; it could be huge."

I hoped she wasn't disappointed that I hadn't signed us up as a duet. Lucille did have a strong voice, but I wanted the spotlight all for myself.

She lived with her grandma and two older brothers around the corner from us in the coloured district. According to my Mom Lucille's family were as 'black as the ace of spades.' Everyone said that Negroes had rhythm and could sing and dance better than white folks.

I know I loved to listen to the congregation whooping it up during the Saturday service at the nearby Baptist Church that Lucile's family attended. Their music was loud and exciting. It didn't sound anything like the tired hymns from the Catholic Church where I went.

"Lucille, can anyone in your family play the piano for me? I have to practise every day this week. My audition is next Saturday"

"My brother Jerry can play. He's really good, and besides, he has a crush on you. I'll go ask him."

Jerry was two years older than I was and I thought he was kinda cute. He was shy and didn't talk much, which was okay, since I only needed him to play the piano.

I overheard Jerry say, "Are you sure she can sing?"

I couldn't hear Lucille's answer so I guess she must have whispered or used sign language. He shrugged his shoulders as he reluctantly agreed to give me a hand, starting the next day.

"Lucille, will you go with me in the morning to the thrift store to help me pick out my outfit?"

"Sure. I'll tag along with you. It'll be fun."

After two hours of searching we found the perfect outfit waiting for me. The price was right and my Mom should be able to alter the jeans from a size 12 to a size 6 without any problem.

I was going to look super-hot in the tightened jeans and baggy plaid shirt. The kid-size 'Roy Rogers' cowboy hat was a bit too small for my big head, but it would be okay. My brother's Western-style boots could complement my signature look. No one would know they didn't belong to me after I stuffed the toes with Kleenex.

Lucille loved my new duds, but she thought it best not to change my stage name to Hiawatha until after I was discovered.

The next stop was Heinzman's music shop to buy the sheet music for Your Cheating Heart. Joni James recorded it and this song made it to number one on the hit parade. My rendition would also make me a star.

This was the first time I had seen a musical score and I wondered what all the black signs meant on the white sheet. My old song books had the lyrics of the top forty tunes, but they didn't have any classy black marks in them.

Our sessions started that afternoon after Grandma Foster gave me a huge toothless grin. She was as dark and wrinkled as a dried prune, with a head of gray hair like steel wool, and she always wore the same tired housedress.

I could tell she was happy to see me when she said, "Nancy, you're just in time. I baked some of your favourite biscuits."

Grandma Foster was a good cook and always had something delicious to eat; plus we didn't have to wash the dishes when we were finished. Her heavy biscuits with white, thick gravy on top were the best. She treated me like family and always took time to listen to my singing without saying a word about it.

Practising was all work and not much fun especially when Jerry couldn't find the right key. He always kept his head down and never once gave me eye contact, sort of like he was embarrassed about something. He sometimes looked at Lucille and rolled his eyes like it was my fault.

I figured he was probably afraid to look at me because he was in love with me. Or maybe he really wasn't a good musician after all. But it was too late to hire a professional. Jerry might get better.

The best part of that week was spending countless hours with Lucille's family in their old house, a white-washed bungalow with loads of junk right in the front yard. It looked like an abandoned service station with treadless tires and various rusted auto parts strewn among bits of dry grass.

The few windows were covered with yellowing bed-sheets and the unpainted wooden front steps were rotted and wobbly. No one cared if I took off my shoes when I came inside.

Jerry continued to roll his eyes whenever I couldn't hit his note. After four days of this abuse it dawned on me that maybe he was trying to tell me something. Perhaps I didn't sound anything like Joni James. The harder I tried the worse I became. Advice came from every corner.

Mom said. "You're spending too much time at Lucille's place, and not enough time on your homework."

Lucille told me to relax and use my hands and hips more. She thought standing up straight just didn't fit the mood.

"You're too rigid and you don't sound like a girl that's just lost her only boyfriend to someone else. For goodness sake, show some emotion."

"You know what? You're a big know-it-all. Shut up and mind your own business."

My dream was turning into a nightmare with no promise of relief. This pressure cooker was getting ready to explode. Two days before show time and I couldn't eat, my stomach hurt and I hated that stupid song and Joni James.

Her forlorn voice was stalking me. Every radio station was playing it. I couldn't get that awful sound out of my head. There was no place to hide and no escape. I wanted to run away from home and forget the whole damn thing.

"I'm sorry, Lucille. I didn't mean it. You're not a know-it-all. I'm the one who thought I was so smart. Let's still be best friends."

"I know you didn't mean it. Why don't we just keep getting together and we can still eat grandma's biscuits and listen to music on the radio."

"Sounds good to me, but I really wish you could sing with me at the audition. I'm scared."

The next day Mom was at her most encouraging.

"Now don't feel bad if you don't make the cut, dear. Remember they can only pick a handful of kids."

Her concern multiplied my own doubts and followed me around every corner. The night before the big debut my restless sleep was filled with nightmares of stage fright and forgotten words.

In the morning Mom took me aside and told me she had changed her mind and couldn't take me to the audition.

"I know you had your heart set on this audition, but I'm just too busy today. The tenants want their beds changed and the floors need washing. Besides the tunnel bus could be crowded and there will probably be hundreds of kids standing in line. I just don't have time. I'm really sorry to let you down."

She looked tired and frustrated when she whispered. "I'll buy you a new outfit or something nice."

I kept silent, even though I wanted to yell Hallelujah!

Mom had to simmer for a long five minutes before I ended our mutual terror.

"Okay. I'll let my big chance go this time. But you have to promise to buy me some tap shoes, a white sequined dance costume, a black top hat and a cane. I really want to take dance lessons and be just like Ginger Rogers and Fred Astaire."

Hush Hush

I realize I'm only twelve, but I wish I could make everything better. I kneel in front of my homemade altar dressed in my big sister's old flannel pajamas. They're baggy, warm and cozy. I begin my evening ritual.

First I make the sign of the cross with holy water then I recite a decade of the rosary. After a year of turmoil I beg the Blessed Virgin to restore peace and harmony to my family.

Ontario's spring struggles to emerge. But life for me is not yet back to the way it used to be when my eighteen-year-old sister and I shared a double bed and cherished memories of happy times like baking cookies and eating popcorn at Saturday afternoon matinees.

Ann never complained about having a kid sister tagging along with her night and day even when she went on a date with her boyfriend.

The upright orange-crate salvaged from the farmers' market serves as an altar for my sanctuary. Standing on end it's covered in pale blue plastic designed to fit this two-tiered wooden container. I was excited when I found it at a downtown dime store, for just 59 cents.

The slit down the center makes it easy to reach inside the rough box. It's an ideal place to hide personal secrets. No one ever looks in there. On top is a small vase containing three artificial yellow roses, a statue of the Virgin Mary, and a collection of holy cards displaying pictures of the baby Jesus and His Mother. Yellow is my favourite colour, but I wish the flowers were fresh so I could smell their sweet, soothing fragrance.

In a trance-like state I stroke the filigree edges of a silver-plated crucifix. The front is smooth and attractive, but the back is hollow and rough. After my prayers I return the cross to its safe hiding spot beside my diary. As usual the memory of a dead baby's funeral rears its ugly head.

The service wasn't held in a Catholic church, and no priest was present to say comforting words of sympathy to the small family gathering. I threaded my way past coats containing people whose faces I couldn't see because their heads were bowed.

A funeral director stood erect at the pulpit. He avoided eye contact when he mumbled a short, irrelevant passage from the Bible.

I needed an explanation, but none was given. I thought it was strange that my mother hadn't read about this death in the daily newspaper. Mom's mission was to always keep our family informed of every obituary, whether we wanted to hear about it or not.

Whose baby is this? How did it die? Am I the only one kept in limbo here?

I heard two old ladies whisper, "What a shame. But it's a blessing in disguise, and probably for the best. They're too young to care for a child anyway."

In spite of the dozen or so mourners, the back room of Janisse Brother's Funeral Home felt empty, stale and silent with the cold dead air. A lone bouquet of pink chrysanthemums was the only hint of life.

Any hope of escape was stifled by the windowless, slate-coloured room.

A tiny wooden coffin was draped with white velvet, like a scarf, tasseled with limp gold threads. A small silver cross sat in the middle of the cloth.

I shuddered as I imagined the rigid body of an infant lying inside this simple container.

I couldn't help myself from staring at Ann, my teenage sister. She was wearing a too-large, matronly black suit that belonged to Mom. Her pill-box hat with a droopy veil did little to hide her red, bleary eyes.

Dark leather gloves couldn't conceal those trembling hands. This couldn't be my sister. She looked old, more like a middle-aged woman. What happened to my vibrant, fun-loving idol?

Oh, my God. Could this be her baby?

I remembered when Mom told me, "Ann has gone to help your Aunt Hazel. There's no phone on the farm so you can't call her. Don't worry, she'll be home soon."

But high school graduation and prom night had come and gone without Ann. I felt so alone without her. Mom and Dad tried to keep me busy, but they were no substitute for my lively best friend.

When she finally came home that fall she seemed somehow different and very tired. Her usual sparkling blue eyes looked dull and swollen, and that contagious smile of hers had disappeared.

Now Ann was mourning the death of a child. Her boyfriend, a short Irish lad with red hair and freckles, looked out of place at the funeral. His old man's starched white shirt, striped tie and black pants didn't suit him.

Where were his familiar faded blue-jeans? Was he the father?

Without music the awkward silence was broken by quiet sobs of despair. I later found out that life and death must have been beyond their control since their baby girl had only survived for a few short months.

The two families pretended not to feel anger or blame as they babbled amongst themselves. This was a personal family matter; no one on the outside had to know.

The service was over, the damage was done. Their innocent crime had been punished.

Pushing back tears Ann gave me the silver cross for safe-keeping as she whispered, "You understand, don't you?"

Without looking at her or being sure what we were talking about, I answered, "Yes."

Somehow I knew it was best to hide the cross inside my altar. We never spoke of the cross again or baby Janet.

Our unspoken oath of secrecy was made. All my unanswered questions would have to wait.

In the meantime, I drifted through the hush of the fog and pretended that everything was okay.

Seeing through Blue Eyes

Everything was different after that day. I wanted to wake up a carefree, happy fourteen-year old teenager again with nothing better to do than call my girlfriends and talk for hours.

My Mom ran a rooming house in our home to help with the bills during tough times like when Dad was in jail or on a binge. Every Saturday morning it was my job to collect the rent, wash the floors, and help Mom change the beds.

I always looked forward to my pay day when the chores were finished. After lunch my best friends and I would walk five blocks to catch the tunnel-bus to downtown Detroit. We giggled and laughed during the ten minute ride in anticipation of window-shopping and spending all of our Canadian money.

I loved to buy new clothes in the States, especially Levi jeans. They weren't just any jeans; they were the authentic brand with the famous red tab on the edge of the right back pocket.

Most times I was also on the hunt to find something pretty to match whatever I had bought the previous week. The bargains and styles were always better in Detroit than in Windsor, or at least that's what we wanted to believe.

It was a time of fun, laughter and lighthearted day-dreams interrupted only by homework and boring classes.

School was easy for me even though I was a year younger than the kids in my class. My parents were happy that I had decided to go to a Catholic middle school for Grades 9 and 10, and I was relieved that it was for girls only since I was bashful around boys.

In Grade 10, I was shocked when Mother Agnes took me aside and told me I had been chosen to portray the Blessed Virgin Mary on our school's float in the May Day Parade.

I overheard some of the girls talking in the hallway between classes.

"Why would the nuns pick her? She's so skinny and shy."

"I think they chose her because she went to Mass every day during Lent, and besides she gave up eating sweets for the whole forty days."

Another beauty swished her blonde ponytail as she said, "Maybe because she's a goodie-goodie who happens to look like the statue of Mary in the hall. Her baby blue eyes and long brown hair are a perfect match for the real McCoy."

One of the most popular girls gave her opinion.

"She doesn't go out with boys so of course she was chosen."

Whatever the reason; I wasn't given a choice.

In Windsor the May 1st holiday in honour of Mary the Mother of God was a huge celebration for Catholics. All the schools and various societies took part parading down Ouellette Avenue to Jackson Park. Thousands of the faithful marched or lined the sidewalks to watch marching bands, and colourful religious floats glide past.

I was anchored to a post on the flatbed of a semi-truck by a belt hidden under my long, light-blue flowing gown and long shawl. My head was completely covered by a matching head scarf. This entire garb came from the Ursuline nuns who taught at our school.

My costume was probably left over from some nativity scene or a long-past Christmas concert. During the procession I desperately wanted to run away, but I couldn't move.

I was stuck there for what seemed like an eternity surrounded by a blanket of pure white 'Kleenex carnations' that everyone at school had helped make to decorate our float.

As I fingered the beads of my oversized rosary I prayed for this horror show to end quickly. I managed to get through the two-hour journey by keeping my eyes down and not looking at the crowds gathered on the sidewalk.

But I'm quite sure I heard my brother shout, "Smile, Fancy Nancy, with the onion ears and carrot nose."

I didn't realize that while I was parading about town making a fool of myself Mom was having my bedroom painted a sunny shade of yellow. The drab room was suddenly converted into a bright and cheerful space perfect for a blossoming teen. Somehow Mom always seemed to know surprises made me happy.

The new look helped me to forget all about my humiliating day, and soon I felt almost back to normal.

Because the paint fumes were strong, Mom suggested I sleep on the couch in our living room for a couple of nights. She said she didn't mind the smell. She knew my eyes were sensitive and she wanted me to have a good night's rest after my exhausting day.

No sooner had I got to sleep than I was startled by Mom yelling out Dad's name. I ran into my bedroom to see what was going on.

"Joe, Blue Eyes is jerking off outside Nancy's window!"

"That son of a bitch. I'm going to get my gun out of the closet and scare the shit out of him before I beat his head in."

"Don't be crazy, Joe. He'll report you and you'll be the one to get arrested and end up back in jail."

"Nancy," she screamed. "Go back to the living room right now."

But I couldn't move.

Mom told me that around midnight she had suffered with relentless hot flashes and couldn't sleep. In addition to the night sweats she was also tormented by Dad's steady snoring. To get some relief, she had moved to my empty bedroom.

Just as she was getting comfortable she heard a peculiar noise outside my window like a shower of pebbles hitting against the glass. Without turning on the light, she crept over to the window to take a peek. There was our roomer, a guy Mom had nicknamed Blue Eyes, tossing tiny stones with one hand, while the other hand was busy toying with his private parts.

Little did he know his audience was his landlady and not her teenage daughter.

Blue Eyes had disappeared by the time Dad ran out to the back yard. He quickly called the police, but the officer on duty told him there wasn't anything they could do unless they were able to catch the suspect in the act.

Dad decided he would wait until the next day to settle the score, without any help from the so-called law enforcement authorities.

At breakfast Mom whispered to me. "Nancy, don't you worry. Your dad will deal with him today."

I didn't say a word. All I could do was stare out the bay window in our kitchen alcove and look at the withered daffodils in the flower bed in our backyard. All the while I fiddled with the silk scarf I always wore around my neck to cover an ugly mole.

How long had he been watching me? Were other men undressing me with their eyes? Why didn't I think to always close the blinds? Was it my fault? I shouldn't have worn tight jeans. I'm so embarrassed. Why do men want to expose themselves anyway? Please, God, let me wake up from this nightmare and go back to my everyday life. Please don't let Dad hurt him, just make him leave and help me forget.

I never trusted Blue Eyes from the moment he moved into our home, but I didn't share my misgivings with anyone. It wasn't anything he did or said, but more the creepy way he looked at me that made me feel uncomfortable. I also noticed there weren't any pictures of family or friends in his room, and he never received any mail. I felt kind of sorry for the matchstick-skinny guy with his bulging glacier-blue eyes.

He didn't appear to have a life. We didn't know where he worked, or if he even had a job. Mom figured he couldn't be any more than about forty years old. But Blue Eyes was a model tenant: clean, polite and quiet, plus he always paid his rent on time.

Furious and determined, Dad and my two brothers couldn't leave the subject alone. They talked about it non-stop until they conjured up a plan to catch Blue Eyes with 'his pants down.'

They decided they would hide behind the garage after dark and when he started his performance they would move in and beat him to a pulp.

I overheard my brother say, "It'll serve him right, the God-damned pervert".

Mom let Dad and the boys plan their revenge while she listened to my cry for help.

"Please don't let them hurt him," I pleaded. "I just want the whole thing to go away. I can't stand to hear any more about Blue Eyes."

She spoke with her usual wisdom.

"Don't you worry. We're going to take care of everything."

She insisted that the two of us confront the creep. She made me go up the stairs with her. I was shivering uncontrollably.

Mom knocked on his door while I kept my eyes glued to the dirty carpet.

When Blue Eyes opened the door she said in a low but firm voice, "Pack up your things and get the hell out."

"What do you mean, Mrs Yager? What's the problem? I paid my rent yesterday."

"You know exactly what I'm talking about. Now get moving, and leave Nancy alone. I'm warning you, if you don't go right now my husband is about to go crazy and he's liable to kill you."

I watched as he got into the taxi and slowly drove away, his icy blue eyes fixed on me.

He was gone, but he never left.

Mercy

"Applications are being accepted. Oppressed by a fatal disease, a severe handicap, or a crippling deformity? Write Box 264, Royal Oak, Michigan. Show proper compelling medical evidence that you should die, and Dr. Jack Kevorkian will help you kill yourself free of charge."

The words 'kill yourself free of charge' sent a chill through me. I was ripped apart, both repulsed and fascinated when I read this ad that had appeared in a Detroit newspaper.

Death always fills me with fear and anxiety, especially the thought of losing loved ones. I'm in good company when I admit to being obsessed with death and dying. I follow in the shadow of Jack Kevorkian, Sue Rodriguez, Robert Latimer and my brother Joey.

Joey came from a completely different background than Dr. Kevorkian, the son of Armenian immigrants, but shared the same viewpoint when it came to assisted suicide. They believed no one should have to suffer a long, painful death.

Kevorkian's keen interest in death started after he graduated from medical school with a specialty in pathology. His images of the eyes of dying patients earned him the nickname 'Doctor Death.' He photographed the retina of their eyes at the exact moment of death. He did this in the hope of distinguishing between death and coma. Kevorkian discovered that the corneas became invisible at this critical moment.

His intimate contact with the dying confirmed his belief that a physician's duty is to help eliminate pain and suffering especially in the chronically and terminally ill. For the next half-century, Kevorkian devoted himself to his dream of a system of suicide clinics that would allow doctors to participate in compassionate medically-planned deaths.

Kevorkian designed and built a suicide machine that allowed a user to self-inject a narcotic, followed by a lethal dose of potassium chloride. His machine enabled candidates for suicide to kill themselves at the mere touch of a button.

Several clients also expired in his 1968 Volkswagen bus, which he had rigged with equipment to induce carbon monoxide poisoning. He was determined to test the law in order to change it.

My brother also challenged the law. The first time Joey came out of prison he was only eighteen, but now he wore the 'jailbird label' for vehicular manslaughter.

In his defense Mom said that he regretted driving his car while drunk, and causing the accident that killed a young motorcyclist.

Mom used to say, "Joey, you're the smartest one in this family. If only you'd apply yourself and stop bucking the law."

Joey never followed her advice.

His formal education was replaced with lessons on pain, suffering and the need for compassion, all learned during his times in Guelph Reformatory. After his first stint he was sentenced again for theft, break-and-entry, and possession of stolen goods.

At one point Dad was locked-up at the same time and confided to Mom that the guards used a large leather strap called the 'Paddle' to keep guys in line. Joey was on the receiving end of up to ten strokes each time.

Dad was haunted by the nightmare of his son stripped naked and attached to an upright frame in a bent position, his hands and legs clamped. The inmates referred to this device, located in what they called the Limbo Room, as 'The Machine.' It was used to cause pain and suffering, whereas Kevorkian's suicide machine brought terminal pain and suffering to a peaceful end.

The Paddle did nothing to change Joey's conduct; rather it made him a little cockier, and more belligerent. Dad believed his physical pain was less traumatic than the indignity of being forced to drop his trousers, and pull his shirt over his head so he couldn't identify the person inflicting the punishment.

Embarrassed and humiliated, he was at the mercy of sadistic guards. Out of pride, Joey felt it was important not to cry or scream or beg, as so many did. But deep down where it really counted, he was hurting.

After his release he worked as a truck driver. He felt respected on the job and later he relished the status earned when he was elected as a union representative.

A serious back injury forced him to quit his job and go on Worker's Compensation. But Joey's 'money-for-nothing' settlement did more harm than good.

Two botched back operations stripped him of purpose and left him instead with a metal rod up his back and a ton of pain medication. With no job and nothing to tweak his interest Joey's new addictions became watching TV and drinking beer.

Joey had already lost Dad. He hadn't expected to lose our brother Pete, his confidant and best friend, to a damaged heart.

Now he was the only male left in the family. Perhaps Joey felt responsible for Mom and his sisters when he began his dangerous dabbling with assisted suicide and euthanasia.

Mom never told anyone she wanted to die, and in fact she wasn't in much physical pain. A series of mini-strokes left her brain activity out of sync. Her 88-year old body reduced her from a chubby five foot woman to an even shorter 85-pound shell.

She didn't recognize her kids, couldn't feed herself and could only say a few words. Yet Joey knew, or thought he knew that she wanted to end her life in the nursing home where she was held prisoner.

Like Kevorkian, he looked into Mom's eyes and decided they were the eyes of the dying. Probably she swallowed the rice pudding without noticing Joey's hands tremble as he spoon-fed her a concoction of his own painkillers.

The dose was too small to kill Mom.

His failed attempt to end her life went unnoticed by her caregivers. Joey only told one person about his botched euthanasia plan.

Me.

"I didn't want to kill Mom, but I couldn't stand by and watch her suffer so much indignity. You know she's always been proud and independent."

Mom died a few months later of natural causes without anyone other than the two of us knowing of her previous brush with death.

Joey continued to follow and defend the work of Dr. Kevorkian, fully supporting the idea that no one should suffer prolonged and agonizing pain from a chronic or terminal illness.

Joey sometimes referred to himself jokingly as Dr. Death. He and Kevorkian even resembled each other with oversize glasses perched on the end of their long noses. Without a doubt, he preferred to be called a doctor rather than a kind-hearted drunk.

Throughout the '90s Kevorkian challenged the authorities to legalize his actions or find a way to stop him. In order to effect change, he needed his audience to pay attention. All his subjects wanted to die and consented to death, either inhaling carbon monoxide or personally activating the suicide machine. To showcase his cause, and in front of a nation of curious voyeurs, Kevorkian administered a lethal injection on CBS's 60 Minutes to a 52-year-old man with Lou Gehrig's disease.

If this was a macabre test to prove the end justifies the means it failed. A jury found the doctor guilty of second-degree murder, since he actively injected the fatal dose. Kevorkian was sentenced to 10-25 years in prison. His actions and the publicity of his trial brought the debate on assisted suicide and euthanasia to the forefront.

With his older brother Pete out of the picture our sister Betty became Joey's best buddy, but before long poor health and incurable emphysema forced her into isolation.

I can imagine Betty sitting on the toilet in her windowless bathroom taking just one more drag. Life without freedom, closeted in a small space and unable to go outside, was pure torture for her, as Joey knew all too well.

Betty pleaded with her doctor and anyone who would listen.

"I want to die. Please let me die."

Joey performed one final favour for Betty by most likely giving her enough painkillers to successfully end her life. To ensure he didn't screw up again he turned off her oxygen tank and covered her unconscious face with a plastic grocery bag. She died in peace while Joey held her hand.

Unlike Betty, Sue Rodriguez was the first Canadian female to fight for the right to end her life.

"If I cannot give consent to my own death," she asked, "Whose body is this? Who owns my life?"

In 1992, Sue Rodriguez forced the right to die debate into the Canadian spotlight. Diagnosed with Lou Gehrig's disease, she asked the lawmakers to change the statute banning assisted suicides, but the Supreme Court ruled against her. She committed suicide in 1994 with the help of an anonymous doctor who wasn't afraid to take a chance.

In failing health, Kevorkian was granted parole from prison in 2007. He had helped more than 130 terminally or chronically ill patients take their own lives. He emerged from prison in poor health, totally unrepentant, and still determined to effect change.

If Joey were around today, he would be defending not only Kevorkian and Rodriguez, but also Robert Latimer. This farmer from Saskatchewan murdered his disabled daughter by placing her in the cab of his truck and letting exhaust fumes take her life.

Tracey Latimer was born suffering from severe cerebral palsy. She never developed control over her extremities or any ability to feed herself or sit upright. When a third operation was proposed for the 13 year-old, the attending surgeon was not convinced that Tracy had the strength to survive, nor was there any guarantee her pain would be lessened.

How can a father stand by and watch his little girl suffer without any hope of a cure? Jurors found Latimer guilty of second-degree murder in 1994, but the Supreme Court eventually nullified the conviction. A second guilty verdict was later upheld.

I can imagine Joey saying, "The poor sucker should be able to go home. He isn't a criminal, for Christ's sake."

Joey thought it strange that we are kinder to animals than we are to humans. He believed no one in his or her right mind would allow a beloved pet to endure a slow death racked with pain and suffering.

The last time I saw my brother he was on top of a sterile, white sheet in a single hospital bed with rigid chrome bars on each side. When he caught me staring at his grotesque feet, he laughed. The dry, pink stumps were swollen to double their normal size. Joey managed to wiggle his toes in a last gesture of humour. Excess fluid had also collected in his heart and lungs, but lucky for me, I couldn't see inside his scrawny body.

Three months later on Father's Day, Joey's body was discovered in his cockroach-infested apartment. The autopsy report read, 'The excessive amount of drugs in his system may have been his attempt to control the pain'.

Social values and the law are slow to change. Corporal punishment designed to cause pain and suffering like Joey endured in prison no longer threatens others. The use of the strap was abolished in Canada in 1972.

Robert Latimer was granted full parole on November 29th 2010 after spending seventeen years in jail.

Jack Kevorkian's life story became the subject of the 2010 movie 'You Don't Know Jack' which earned actor Al Pacino an Emmy and Golden Globe Award for his portrayal of Kevorkian.

After the awards Jack said, "You'll hear people say, it's in the news again, it's time for discussing this further. No it isn't. It's been discussed to death. There's nothing new to say about it. It's a legitimate ethical medical practice as it was in ancient Rome and Greece."

Jack Kevorkian died from natural causes without assistance on June 3rd 2011 in a Detroit hospital. The time has now come to finally vindicate Dr. Death as well as others like Sue Rodriguez, Robert Latimer and my brother, Joey.

Special Delivery

It was now five in the morning as I tossed and turned trying to figure out why I couldn't sleep. Was it food poisoning from something I ate? Or was it my husband's incessant snoring that was pissing me off?

I felt fat, scared and run-down. Over Christmas I had eaten too much, slept too little and was carrying an extra thirty-five pounds. Thank God I only had one more month until my due date. Getting out of our double bed, I pulled on my tired stretch pants, a long-sleeved flannel top and lamb's-wool slippers.

Nothing could be seen through the frosted window that early in the morning darkness, but I heard a howling wind ripping through the frozen trees. A cold snap was breaking all-time records in Windsor. I was sick and tired of our brutal Ontario weather, and of holiday preparations, and the heavy weight I was forced to lug around.

Our three daughters were asleep and snuggled up in cozy blankets at the end of the hall in the other upstairs bedroom. I tiptoed down the creaky stairs careful to keep my balance, allowing my bulging stomach to take the lead. It would be good to get an early start to another busy day and doing some chores left over from the holidays might take my mind off my woes.

With a new found burst of energy I decided to give the kitchen a good scouring. Mom had taught me to always scrub the floors on my hands and knees as she believed sponge mops were 'good for nothing.' Lysol promised to get rid of 99.9% of unsuspecting germs so I poured the liquid into my scrub bucket along with steaming hot water.

I attacked every minute trace of dirt and grime under the table and in all the hard to reach corners with a stiff scrub brush, stopping every few minutes to ease my aching back and to take some deep breaths. I was an enormously fat woman on a mission. Every inch of the geometric mosaic pattern of the old linoleum was transformed into show home condition before I stopped. It looked so damned good I felt like eating my breakfast off the floor, but the antiseptic smell stopped me.

After this grueling workout I felt entitled to a reward, but I couldn't relax as everything felt out of kilter. My favorite Colombian coffee tasted bitter and even the daily newspaper didn't interest me. The horoscope and fashion section along with the grocery flyers were somehow dull and lackluster.

I stared at the clock and timed the false, but intense contractions. They were six minutes apart. Angry jabs were traveling from my belly to the small of my back. Between spasms I forced myself to wash my hair in the kitchen sink before I trudged back up the fourteen steps to our bedroom.

"Wake up, Glenn. Don't panic, but I've been having false labor pains for a couple of hours."

His voice was groggy when he said, "Maybe you should pack your bag, just in case."

"Don't be silly. I'll just go back downstairs and lie on the couch. No sense waking the kids; they were up late last night."

Perhaps twenty-nine was too old to be having another baby. My daughters seemed to believe so, and at eight, seven, and five they were the experts. I stopped working as a realtor just one week before Christmas when the doctor told me that my due date should be at the end of January.

This couldn't be real labour. I wasn't ready and besides it was too early. I didn't have any baby clothes, diapers or even bottles. I was looking forward to a month of shopping and relaxing.

Going to the hospital wasn't in my day-timer. I didn't want to cry wolf only to be sent home in embarrassment. Besides no kid would want to have their birthday the day before New Year's Eve so close to Christmas. I would feel cheated if my gifts were combined into one celebration.

The stairs had become steeper as I gripped the handrail all the way down to the living room. Taking a slight detour before going to the couch, I crossed over the now gleaming floor, and made my way into our telephone-booth sized half-bathroom adjoining the kitchen.

Glenn didn't waste any time getting shaved, showered and dressed for work in his suit, white shirt and tie. He made up his mind to stay home, at least for awhile.

He remembered my past routine of constant denials whenever there was an emergency. Mom always said I had a one track mind and he knew from experience it was senseless to argue with me. He also realized timing was critical since all three girls were delivered in near record time.

Coming into the kitchen Glenn noticed I was in the bathroom.

"Is everything okay in there?"

"I'm fine. I just feel constipated."

He had heard this line before our last daughter Valerie was born. He tried to reason with me to come out and go to the hospital, but soon gave up his futile plea.

I heard him lift the phone and dial. His strained voice was low, yet explicit and clear.

"Send an ambulance as fast as you can to 304 Belle Isle View. My wife is in labor and I'm sure it'll be quick."

"Hang up that damn phone. I don't want an ambulance for God's sake, and I'm not going to the hospital."

He hung up, just as I yelled, "My water broke!"

My usual slow-moving, conservative husband changed into a madman who wanted to be boss. In a flash, he transformed himself from a reserved Clark Kent to a raving Superman who tried to yank me off my throne.

"I won't let you have our baby in the toilet. Now either you get up or I'm going to drag you out."

He was obsessed, and in such a hurry that I never had time to pull up my stupid pants. This insane tug-of-war ended at the narrow passage near the top of the basement staircase.

The girls crept down from upstairs to see what all the noise was about. They were frightened since we were both always quiet and under control. They had never heard us yelling at each other.

Glenn shouted for Lori, our second oldest daughter, to put on a coat and run over to get help from the lady across the street. Jo-Anne had five kids and would know what to do.

"Tell her your Mom is having the baby."

Next he yelled at Glenda to take her five-year-old sister Val upstairs and keep her there.

Jo-Anne arrived dressed in a winter jacket thrown over her tattered terry cloth housecoat and instructed Lori to go upstairs with her sisters. Jo-Anne gripped my hands, and lied that everything would be okay. She said it could take some time before the baby would come.

Still standing in the narrow hallway, I straddled the germ-free linoleum. One more final push and then BINGO. A wet, sticky lump slid down between my legs.

I cried, "The baby's here!"

Slow motion Glenn clicked into turbo speed and made the precision catch before our new arrival hit the bundled-up slacks that cuffed my ankles. I stood fixed in my own unfocused world.

"Congratulations, you have daughter number four."

In my stupor I almost said, "How can you tell?"

Then her sudden piercing cry filled me with joy.

She was alive! I could see a head covered with black hair, two arms, two legs, and puckered skin, chalky with a pinkish hue, all encased in a thin, slippery mucus. It was, and still is, the best experience of my life.

I felt elated, fearless, and wildly happy. Adrenalin galloped through my shaking body as we stood huddled together waiting for help to arrive. Nothing would ever be able to tear us apart.

Giddy with excitement, I felt there was now no need to go to the hospital, but when I heard the shrill sirens in the driveway I knew I didn't have a choice. Running around the block in my euphoric state would have to wait for another time.

I pictured the Keystone Cops when two male attendants managed to get their stretcher wedged in our side entrance. The wide-open door created a wind tunnel as we stood frozen in the hallway. Glenn was holding our still naked baby while he pinched the umbilical cord that had broken in half.

My teeth were chattering and I couldn't stop shaking. All the while, my long fingernails were digging into the back of Jo-Anne's hand.

Glenn gave this last order to the men.

"Run around to the front door. It's wider and the stretcher should fit."

"Yes, sir. Now you go and boil some water for us. We'll take care of everything."

It was tempting to laugh out loud at this crazy idea, but I managed to control myself.

After tying off the cord they wrapped her burrito-style in a clean white towel. My twitching body was loaded onto the stretcher, and gently covered with a red wool blanket. Baby-burrito was placed in an incubator at the front of the ambulance. I was delegated to the back of the bus while Glenn was told to make his own way to Hotel Dieu Hospital.

The pots filled with boiling water were left untouched to clutter the stove. I guessed no one had time to make a cup of tea. Our neighbor cleaned up the bloody mess on the once spotless floor, and watched the girls until my mother could come over.

Flying down the city streets I listened to the non-stop deafening screech of the siren and gruff voices talking on a mobile radio.

"We're on our way. Mother and newborn appear to be stable. Anticipate arrival in fifteen minutes."

Appear to be stable? Wild thoughts took over my mind... *Maybe my baby won't be fine. Maybe she'll die. Our life will never be the same. What if there's brain damage? How can I tell the girls? Why didn't I go to the hospital sooner? I'm so dumb.*

Common sense or reason finally took hold. I heard myself say, "Take us to the nearest hospital. Forget Hotel Dieu. Go to Metropolitan Hospital and hurry up."

Once again the driver dialed the phone.

"Patient now wants to change hospitals. Alert staff at Metropolitan. We'll be at the emergency entrance in five minutes."

No one informed Glenn of my change in venues. He later told me that he felt like a fool, and probably resembled a mass murderer, when he ran into Hotel Dieu, in his blood-spattered business suit, demanding to see his wife and new daughter.

By the time Glenn and I were re-united I had settled down and accepted that our baby would have to be kept in isolation for twelve hours. Home births were frowned upon, and the staff had to make sure that she wouldn't contaminate the other babies in the nursery.

My Lysol argument didn't seem to make any difference to them.

Carrying a dozen yellow roses, Glenn gave me a gentle kiss and asked, "How's our little Heather doing?"

"Sorry, that's not her name. I know we agreed on Heather, but I've changed my mind. Her name can't be Heather. A mysterious voice in my head told me she must be called Beth, not Elizabeth, just Beth. I promise there won't be any more battles, and I'll stop being a stubborn bitch, if you accept this change."

"Okay, if it's that important, but I've already called everyone and told them the news. The kids think they have a sister named Heather."

The new name came out of nowhere, without any previous consideration. It just popped into my head, but it was non-negotiable.

Five weeks passed before the shock started to recede. Friends and family rallied around us with beautiful baby clothes, gifts and everyday necessities. The girls loved their new sister and soon became her surrogate mothers.

Glenn took pleasure in joking that he could now add Certified Midwife to his resume. I gradually got back to my crazy antics following in the footsteps of Lucille Ball.

Folie a Deux

We sip a distinctive Napa Valley Cabernet Sauvignon in the intimate Manresa Castle Restaurant in Port Townsend Washington, a celebration of our 30th wedding anniversary.

Both of us are in the mood to have some fun after long days and nights trying to sell property to bargain hunters, and babysitting impatient sellers during a slow real estate market at home in the Okanagan Valley.

Glenn says, "Let's treat ourselves to an expensive bottle of red wine for a change."

The 'Folie a Deux' label captures his attention with its Rorschach interpretation of black dancing figures. The description on the menu was enough to convince us to splurge and pay $30 for the pleasure.

Good structure and balance, combined with complex layers of chocolate blended with blackberry and black cherry. The tannins form a lasting finish while allowing the unique flavors to maintain their individuality.

We're sold.

Memories explode in our space as we laugh out loud about our youth, a time when we believed, like the Pope, that we were infallible. To go along with our Folie a Deux we order a char grilled filet mignon topped with brandy demi-glace before we peek at the dessert list with mouth-watering anticipation.

In so many ways our marriage has been a true 'folie a deux.' We've always shared the same delusions right from the time we met at our Catholic High School in Windsor, Ontario. I was sixteen and Glenn was seventeen when we started dating after eyeing each other in church at our annual school retreat.

Gas for his Dad's '49 Meteor cost 29 cents a gallon and since Glenn was always broke, and I never offered to pay, we would park on the main street and talk for hours.

My mother didn't buy into his plight. She thought Glenn was cheap, and didn't know how to treat her youngest daughter properly.

Our typical conversation, usually a lively debate, might include topics on religion, psychology, family behavior, movies, school or almost anything that came into our heads.

"Can you believe that Mother Gerald sent me home to change my skirt? What a bag. Who cares if I didn't want to wear my uniform for one day out of the year? It's not like it's a mortal sin. By the way, did your Mom chew you out for flunking Grade 13?"

"Naw, she still won't talk about it. She can't swallow the idea that her perfect son gets straight As one year and fails the next. I think she has started a novena for me and prays that I win a scholarship next year."

While we clink our glasses and propose another toast to our health, wealth and happiness the waiter arrives with the main course proudly presented on a silver platter.

Glenn embarrasses me when he tells the waiter, "This beats the hell out of York frozen meat pies, my wife's signature dish."

"Don't listen to him. That was my specialty when I was twenty years old. Now I'm Martha Stewart in disguise."

Glenn rolls his eyes.

We don't waste any time before we savour the medium rare meat enhanced by Folie a Deux.

I can't keep my mouth shut for long.

"Remember those love letters you sent to me while I was in teacher's college?"

"How could I forget? But your letters were like reading the newspaper or watching Dragnet. 'Just the facts, ma'am, just the facts'."

"My biggest shock was when you proposed to me at the show during Alfred Hitchcock's Psycho. I thought you looked a bit like Anthony Perkins when he butchered Janet Leigh in the shower. Nevertheless I said yes and took a chance on my destiny."

"I have to admit I came close to killing you a few times. Like when I trusted you to let out the pants of my expensive new suit. That was a big mistake. My Mom or any one of my five sisters would have known not to use a razor blade to open up a tight seam."

"That was smart of me. You never asked me again to sew or iron anything for you."

Our wine seems to vanish quickly as we listen to the echo of footsteps from ghosts that still live in this hotel, a former Jesuit Seminary.

To hell with the cost, we break down and each order a glass of their cheap house wine.

Jumping back to our wedding we begin reminiscing. We actually believed that our big day was for us to enjoy. That was a joke.

We could have eloped, but then we would have missed seeing your white tuxedo jacket worn with the too-short black trousers. Your new white sports socks somehow didn't convey the dignified image we intended, nor did my $25 second-hand wedding gown.

But the photos taken by family and friends provided us with many years of laughs. The old saying, 'pictures don't lie' was indeed the truth.

We begged our friends and family to give us cash rather than gifts. Everyone obliged us except for Mike, our good friend. After we harassed him non-stop he reluctantly agreed to buy us something practical: a box spring and mattress.

Our wedding turned into a fiasco when we unexpectedly couldn't get married at eleven in the morning at the parish church we had chosen. It was hastily re-scheduled for nine at another church.

However, we stood by our culinary wisdom and stuck with their lunch menu of hot beef sandwiches with French fries smothered in rich brown gravy. We knew our favourite chocolate-covered 'long johns' would make an excellent finale.

There was no way we would change our minds about the menu and have a traditional breakfast. Why would we agree to pay $1.25 for a boring plate of bacon and eggs when we could have a gourmet feast for .75 cents a head at the CANUSA restaurant across from the Chrysler truck plant?

I remember my sister saying, "I know you had to change your wedding to an earlier time, but it doesn't mean you have to insist on still serving that fat-laden meal at ten in the morning, especially at that greasy spoon. You're both out of your minds."

Only a few guests felt sick. The rest told us it was the most unique breakfast ever. Along with all the compliments our best man surprised us and picked up the whole twenty dollar tab.

Glenn takes another peek at the Manresa dessert menu, but doesn't see 'long johns' listed.

"I'm going to order the vanilla crème Brule topped with fresh raspberries and you can have one small bite, unless you want your own."

"Just order one. It's expensive, you know. I promise I won't eat it all. I was thinking ... Do you remember the name of the motel in Lima, Ohio where we spent the first night of our honeymoon?"

Glenn never forgets anything.

"The Colonial Motel. But the Bates Motel might have been more appropriate."

The single-storey white clapboard motel looked quaint from the road with its red roof and blood red geraniums in window boxes. The quaintness disappeared instantly when we crossed the threshold. Somehow my expensive silk peignoir set, straight out of Modern Bride, and my matching high heel slippers with fluffy balls of fur at the toe, didn't seem to suit our surroundings.

A vibrating bed gave us five minutes of shakes and uncontrolled fits of laughter for one American quarter.

Kneeling down to recite the rosary took fifteen minutes and didn't cost us anything. With anxiety and guarded anticipation we took turns having a shower in the trailer-size tin enclosure until the hot water turned ice-cold and the memory of frenetic discordant sounds and murderous visions filled my head.

Please don't let this be a scene from Psycho.

"I was so darn nervous until you told me to take off my designer nightgown and put on something more comfortable like my shorty pyjamas. What a smart idea since you kept on your white sport socks."

"Do you remember on our way home the next day we stopped at Atlantic Mills in Detroit where we found heaven?"

This brand new discount warehouse was huge with stacks and stacks of bargain-priced clothing, kitchen gadgets, books and prints from around the globe. Almond Joys and Baby Ruth chocolate bars crossed the border along with several bags of bargains. 'Blue Boy and Pinky' Gainsborough prints would complement our living room wall that we planned to paint a striking grape colour.

Soon we could unleash our new-found decorating skills.

Glenn looks down and whispers, "Our two day honeymoon was perfect, and after thirty years I wouldn't trade you for anyone else."

Wow!! I think I'll celebrate and order my own crème Brule.

A week or two after the honeymoon, I was sick every day. It had to be a summer flu that was going around. After nine months and one week I harvested a baby girl we named Glenda.

Teaching elementary school between pregnancies helped support us while Glenn finished his engineering degree. Fifteen months later Lori was born. After another two years Valerie came along.

Our fourth and last daughter, Beth, came out headstrong and determined right on the kitchen floor five years after Val.

Our family was complete.

So many twists and turns in the braided bread-dough of life. Speed bumps at every intersection forced us to slow down for the 'Judder Bars.'

Somehow to us it all made sense.

"I need a coffee to sober up before I start crying. Talking about the good old days makes me sad and sentimental. Besides it's past our bedtime."

Glenn's snoring is constant; it doesn't go away. I can depend on it every single night, but like comfort food I know I will miss it when the shelves are bare. In the meantime our appetites are strong as the 'folie' continues.

Open Wide

Yippee! It's summer and school's out. I feel free and easy like a teenager instead of a thirty-something wife and mother trying to eke out a living as a realtor. The high noon sun brightens my day and for a brief spell it extinguishes any shadows of resentment about having to work.

I manoeuver my '67 Chrysler along the deserted winding roads through manicured cherry and apple orchards. The sweet fragrance of clover and ripening fruit put me into a non-alcoholic high. Relaxed and driving with the windows down I sing along with the Bee Gees to Jive Talkin' blasting from the radio.

Suddenly reality re-asserts itself and I think if only I didn't have to hold another boring open house I could slack off and be free like the rest of my family. I rationalize that it's only a few hours of my time and maybe it will result in a much-needed paycheck.

Anxious sellers greet me at the door.

"Hi, Nancy, it looks like you've got a beautiful day for the open house, but before we leave I'd like you to meet our friend Jack, all the way from England. He's been staying with us."

"Pleased to meet you, Jack. Are you in the market for a house by any chance?"

He shrinks away and raises his bushy eyebrows. Quickly I redeem myself.

"Just kidding, Jack. Go have fun and don't worry about anything. I'll take good care of Queenie."

Queenie, their aging Welsh corgi, watches my every move and follows me as I check all the vertical blinds and heavy draperies to make sure they're open. Next on the list we inspect the bathrooms to ensure the toilet seats are down. Then I wash my hands, and go to the kitchen stove to boil a cinnamon stick, an old real estate trick. Soon the house smells of fresh apple pie.

There's time to arrange some brochures and several of my business cards on the coffee table before the waiting game begins. Queenie keeps constant watch with her sorrowful chocolate-brown eyes.

Based on my experience prospects are more likely to make an offer if they believe there's a lot of interest in the property, so I scratch down a few counterfeit names in the guest book.

Every detail in the house is straight out of the 60s. A new buyer will probably re-invent the place to reflect the current 1975 look. With nothing else to do, I plunk myself down on the dog-haired velour sofa when I spot an oval candy dish filled with my favourite peanut M&Ms on the end table, and wonder how many I can eat without creating a noticeable dent. Limiting myself to two of each of the five colors takes focus and will power. A one-way conversation with my new companion helps pass the time.

"It's no big deal, Queenie, I only had ten of them. I'd give you some, but you're already a too-fat lazy porker."

That's when I accidentally spill the candy all over their outdated orange shag carpet. Queenie's fast, but I manage to save most of them.

Only an hour and a half more before I'll be able to close up and escape. It must be a hundred degrees in the living room when I start to feel clammy and sweaty and can't get comfortable. My Ralph Lauren two-piece business suit is made of wool gabardine lined with polyester, so it doesn't breathe.

I carefully remove my expensive jacket and hang it in the hall closet. I may look good in this starched, long-sleeved blouse and knee-length skirt, but my panty hose are driving me crazy. They're too tight and too short. There's a huge gap between my crotch and the nylons. My hammock-like torture-chamber has got to go. I can't stop tugging at them, but to keep my professional image I mustn't take them off.

Queenie is my only witness when I find some scissors and begin to hack away. It's a relief she can't laugh out loud. I notice a slight glint in her old eyes or is she actually a he? The jagged slit doesn't help much, but at least I have some air circulation.

"Queenie, you're lucky you don't have to wear panty hose. I wish I was a plump, pampered pet like you."

Back on the couch I begin to stare at a huge airborne horsefly making its rounds. It stops for a second on the candy dish before checking out the dining room. A small, mysterious leather box sits seductively to the right of an artificial floral arrangement on the dining room table. The fly continues buzzing above it, circling over and over. I feel compelled to get up and investigate.

As I gingerly lift the top I'm surprised to see an array of shiny dental instruments. The various picks and pliers feel cool to my hot fingers. The four scalars with thin curved blades catch my eye and my interest. I forget about the horsefly and go back to eat another five M&Ms while I ponder my discovery.

I amaze myself with an ingenious idea. It can't be too tough to scale off plaque, and cleaning my own teeth would save me some money and help pass the time.

I've been watching the hygienist every six months for more than twenty years, and after all, my brother-in-law is a dentist. I'm more than qualified for the task. Before anyone comes I'll dig right in and get the job done, but first I've got to put Queenie outside. I don't want an audience while I perform a delicate procedure.

After an initial examination, it's obvious most of the plaque build-up is on the lower incisors. I need some surgical gloves, and a tiny hand mirror would be helpful to see the back molars. After rummaging through several drawers, I can't see any gloves and only find a mirror that's way too large.

Oh well, I'll have to make do and go by feel alone. Finally I'm all set to begin.

Damn it, someone is at the door. I frantically hide the evidence in the lower drawer of the bathroom vanity and put on an enthusiastic smile. The two elderly Jehovah Witness ladies are not interested in seeing the house, but they're definitely committed to saving my soul. Both women are polite and properly dressed in neatly-ironed grey dresses and black lace-up walking shoes. It's tough to get rid of them in a nice way.

I ask if they would mind signing the guest book and come back another time when we could really get into the steps needed for my salvation. They write down their signatures and reluctantly agree to return next Saturday.

At last Mrs Charles Paine and Miss Ivy Wright are on their way out the door. I think their names sound phony, but surely they wouldn't lie.

It's time to get back to my real business before any more interruptions. If I had known I was going to have my teeth cleaned and scaled today, I wouldn't have applied so much fire-engine-red lipstick to my thin lips.

I tackle the lowers first. The pick scraping against plaque is like finger nails on a chalkboard, but I persist. My tongue keeps getting in the way, and I nick it a couple of times. The tomato-tinged saliva mingles with my smudged lipstick, giving the appearance of gigantic fish lips.

After fifteen minutes of intense labor I'm ready for the final test. Sliding my tongue back and forth, over and over, I can't feel any build-up. Uppers and lowers are now smooth and appear to be in good shape. The bleeding at the gum line is minimal; my tongue is functional. I feel proud of my work, and I can't stop smiling in the mirror, although it's a shame about the bright bloodstain on the point of my starched white collar.

Queenie could really use a treatment; her sewer-breath is disgusting. Perhaps if I remove some of the grime and plaque on her teeth it might help, but should I use borrowed precision tools on an animal? What if she decides to chomp off a finger or two? I scrap that idea.

I hadn't thought to sterilize the picks before I started the job, so there's no point in cleaning them now. A quick rinse satisfies my anal compulsion. With loving care, I return the instruments to the box, careful to put the handles down and arrange everything in the same order as I found it. Unless there's a hidden camera in the house, no one will ever know how I spent my time.

Now I treat myself to a few more M&Ms. Gee, they're good. I make one last check of my mouth to make sure there aren't any remnants of chocolate hiding in the crevices. Queenie is whining at the back door.

"Come on in, Queenie dear, and check out my gleaming smile."

It's three in the afternoon and time to close up and take down the signs. On my way out I see the hopeful owners and their friend coming up the driveway.

"Hi, guys. Did you have a nice day?"

"Yeah. We had fun checking out our competition, but nothing on the market compares to our property."

"That's good news. I'm sorry, but it was really slow around here. A few ladies came, but they were just 'lookie-loos.' Maybe I'll try again on a Sunday. It might be better than a Saturday. By the way, how long will you be staying, Jack?"

"I'm leaving tomorrow. I've got to get back to my practice."

"You must be a dentist. I noticed some dental tools on the table."

"Oh, no. I'm a veterinarian. I specialize in treating serious animal diseases. There's a threat of another epidemic of foot and mouth disease in England. We can't take any chances after 1967 when 430,000 animals had to be slaughtered."

"You mean like hoof and mouth disease?"

"Yes, they are the same, but in England we say foot and mouth disease."

Suddenly I feel sick to my stomach, and I'm sure I can feel something like blisters starting to form in my mouth.

"Sorry I've got to run. I'll be here next Sunday, God willing."

I manage to wave goodbye as I screech out of the driveway. At the first twist in the road I pull over to vomit. Fear is working overtime and my internal questions won't quit.

Why didn't I sterilize those stupid instruments? How much time do I have left? Will I have to be put down? Should I tell Glenn or go straight to a doctor?

I vow to give up chocolate and I promise to always practice good dental hygiene if God spares me just this one time.

Please, Lord, I need help. I'm really a good person most of the time.

Cosmic Connections

1. Just Visiting

"What do you mean I'm an alien?"

This so-called psychic must be nuts. Ask anyone who knows me and they'll tell you I'm weird and twisted, but that's hardly grounds for calling me an alien.

Glenn and I were straight arrows from Ontario when we moved to Kelowna in the 70s aiming to meet interesting friends and explore different off-beat paths. I was always interested in psychology and this slowly evolved into dabbling in New-Age thinking including tarot cards, auras, and past lives.

You name it. I did it.

We attended monthly parapsychology meetings at a local hotel for our date night without the kids. Here we heard about Ilse from a lady sitting beside Glenn.

"You guys should meet my girlfriend Ilse from Vernon. She's a real interesting character: an artist and a psychic. She sees auras. She paints watercolour landscapes using the colours she sees in a person's aura."

"That sounds like an interesting combination."

"Granted she's a little different, a bit off the wall, if you know what I mean, but I think she really knows her stuff."

Our first meeting was held at her home in Vernon. A 'GUARD DOG ON DUTY' sign welcomed us. We were too chicken to face the mean-looking pit bull, so we honked the horn and sat in the car until our mystery woman approached.

She was smiling and didn't seem too out of the ordinary for a forty-year old woman wearing a black jogging suit and white high-top running shoes. Her long straight hair was a remnant right out of the 60s, but otherwise she appeared normal, whatever 'normal' means. We shook hands and she invited us inside.

"Come on in and could you please take your shoes off? It's kind of wet outside."

We removed our shoes and carefully danced in stocking feet through the piles of dog crap in the entrance foyer. We were realtors so I was relieved we weren't there to sell the place.

Glenn accepted her offer of a bottle of beer, but declined anything to eat. There wasn't any hocus-pocus talk, or any strange potions boiling in the fireplace. We relaxed and enjoyed an easy exchange sprinkled with the odd joke or two.

In some weird fashion we believed we had connected with Ilse. We commissioned her to do a combined aura painting of us.

Two weeks later she delivered the vibrant art work to our home. We didn't ask her to take off her shoes even though our home was at the opposite end of the spectrum to her rustic place. Strange as it was, we were somehow proud to have the biggest mortgage in town.

We were happy to see painted shades of pumpkin and mustard mingled with splashes of lush green and sea blue on the heavy watercolour paper. I was relieved that she hadn't seen lots of dark shadows with black and grey lines smothered in blood-red as tell-tale signs of our sinful past lives. The painting actually suited our personalities and blended well with our décor.

We sat around the kitchen table and offered her a glass of red wine and a shrimp appetizer. After a couple of glasses of Merlot she blurted out, "By the way, Nancy, you have come from another space. You're an alien."

"You mean like from a different planet?"

She ignored my question and stared at me for a few seconds before she redirected herself.

"You should wear flowing, silky garments and live by water. You will be extremely successful and meet many wealthy international people."

All right. Now you're talking.

"We're in sales," I said, "but so far we haven't met any rich clients."

With a grin on my face and visions of dollars flowing into our bank account I thanked Ilse and invited her to join us for a special coffee spiked with kahlua and topped with whipped cream.

After sharing a little more conversation over coffee, we paid Ilse, said our goodbyes, and decided the alien bit had to be part of her razzmatazz.

For months I tried to bury any eerie thoughts from my consciousness by speculating that our middle-aged psychic friend must have been smoking something harvested on her acreage.

When the hit movie E.T. came out in 1982 I refused to see it and joked that I might see myself or some of my relatives on the giant screen. Although I had dismissed Ilse's far-out comments I kept her vivid watercolour over our toilet so I could always be close to water, forever hopeful that one day her predictions would come true and I would be a wealthy and world-renowned realtor.

Five years flew by before I was reminded that perhaps there was some truth in what Ilse had said.

Cosmic Connections

2. The Thingamajig

"Come on, you two. This camping trip is going to be out of this world."

"Okay, Don, but you know we're not campers, and we don't want to sleep in a tent."

"Don't worry. You won't have to. I borrowed my father's 22-foot fully-equipped Dodge motor home so we could travel and sleep in comfort."

Don and Rose had invited us to join them on this road trip to Wells Gray Park to enjoy the lush fall colours and pure wilderness found at the renowned provincial park. We decided we would leave the kids at home, kick-back, relax and have fun.

The four of us were hyper with anticipation as we planned our get-away from Kelowna. We thought of everything from appetizers, wine and steaks to a hearty breakfast of hash browns, pancakes, bacon and eggs.

In full outdoor gear we headed out of town with Don and Glenn up front in the captain-chairs while Rose and I sat on the back bench. Unlike the men, who were talking business, our conversation ranged from what to do with our hair to the merits of the latest fashions and the annoying behaviour of our teenage daughters. We ultimately decided our kids were in the same category as all typical ungrateful belligerent girls.

Don was our clean-shaven driver and Glenn acted as navigator and co-pilot with his characteristic Smith Brothers black beard. We only stopped once at a service station to check out the bathroom and to evaluate their coffee and sugar donuts.

After four hours of driving we pulled into an entrance marked Dawson Falls Viewpoint and drove to a deserted camping site. We were chomping at the bit to explore and get settled. It was exciting to have the park all to ourselves, just being kids without any agenda or timetable.

There was only one glitch. After getting set up Don turned on the water to test the system, but nothing came out of the tap. The pump wasn't getting any power. The guys were concerned that we wouldn't be able to flush the toilet or have any running water.

A thorough check of the electrical system revealed the problem. I overheard them going on about needing a part, but I didn't have a clue what they were talking about, nor did I care.

Rose asked, "What's wrong?"

Glenn answered, "Nothing, just a burnt-out fuse. We'll need a 30 amp fuse to get the pump going, but we don't feel like driving all the way back to Clearwater to buy one. We can probably rig something up later with tin-foil."

I piped in.

"Let's go down for a walk by the river while the sun is still shining. You can both figure it out later."

Rose and I were lost in our own thoughts as we took the lead. After walking a couple of hundred meters along the river's edge we stopped long enough to take some pictures in front of the falls.

With only rumbling sounds of the water and no conversation it was peaceful to walk mindless through the gravelly sand.

We ambled along side by side until for some unknown reason, I stopped, bent down, and pulled something out of the sand.

Holding the thingamajig between my fingers I turned around to ask my question.

"This isn't what you're looking for, is it?"

Dead silence followed my question. Don and Glenn looked at each other before they stared at me with a dumb look of shocked disbelief.

"Do you even know what a 30 amp automotive fuse looks like?"

"No. Why? Is that what this is?"

Don whispered, "Nancy, you've got to be kidding. This is too freaky. That's a brand-new 30 amp fuse! Was it sticking out of the sand?"

"No."

"Did you feel it under your feet?

"No."

"Oh, come on. Did a voice in your head tell you to bend down?"

"No. I just had the urge."

I thought it was no big deal and wished they would let up on their barrage of questions. All I could think of was a barbecued steak, a glass of red wine and Ilse's words.

"You're an alien."

Cosmic Connections

3. Tuned in.

Talk about a jolt. We didn't see this one coming. Our careers and personal lives were clicking along as well as we could expect, being the owners of a small, non-franchised real estate business in the 1980s and the parents of four daughters.

We invented the name Showtime Realty and gave ourselves the slogan 'Your Family Realtors.' Our somewhat avant-garde staff was more like family with only five realtors and a secretary. Don, our best friend, had worked with us at another firm and later decided to join us at Showtime Realty.

As a team we shared our dreams, hopes and disappointments in a casual, intimate atmosphere. Every Tuesday we met over coffee and doughnuts to brainstorm creative marketing ideas and discuss any new properties we had listed.

On this particular Tuesday Don arrived a few minutes late to find us gathered at our round table in the back office already munching on greasy apple-fritters. Glenn gave him the gears about punctuality and then without thinking about my tone or my words, I blurted out,

"Don, you won't believe the dream I had about you."

"Oh no what did I do?"

"Of all things, I dreamed you were going to quit and go to Re-Max!"

I noticed a slight blush and an almost embarrassed laugh as he answered.

"You know I wouldn't jump ship."

After hearing his reassuring comment I relaxed and was able to get back to work making up innovative marketing ideas. Don left early that day and we didn't see him on Wednesday.

On Thursday he came in and dropped the bomb. He had accepted an offer to go to Re-Max our biggest competitor.

Did I read his mind?

Without any chatter he quickly packed up his belongings and headed towards the back door. He left his swivel leather chair behind for us to use. As he fumbled with the door knob with tears welling up, our secretary started to cry like a sister losing a brother. Maybe she thought our friendship was dead.

A few months passed. We all survived. It wasn't a divorce, but more like a friendly separation.

One early morning after a restless night I called Don to give him hell.

"Hey Don, you know you kept me awake all night."

"And how do you figure that's my fault?"

"I had this awful dream about you."

"Again? What did I do this time?"

"Hold on a minute while I get my coffee."

As I sipped on the bitter dark roast I told him about my nightmare.

"It was mid-afternoon and I could see you at the wheel of 'Seahawk.' You looked like you were stranded somewhere in turbulent waters right in the middle of a fierce storm. Your bulging eyes were like that of a frightened deer. There was no escape, no solution. You were toast, helpless and abandoned. Now can you understand why I couldn't sleep?"

For a second I thought the line was disconnected.

"Hello? Hello? Are you there Don?"

"Jeez, Nancy, you're doing it to me again. I couldn't sleep either so I decided to practise sending out mayday signals. I was studying them to pass the Power Squadron course I'm taking at the Yacht Club."

"You mean I was the one receiving your distress signals?"

"I guess so. Sorry to keep you awake. Next time I'll try to contact someone else to save my life. A realtor who gets lost all the time like you do wouldn't be much help anyway."

"Don, do me a big favour, and turn off this bloody channel."

Cosmic Connections

4. Last Call

I was shivering. My ice-cold fingers and toes felt numb even though it was a warm evening in September. My hands wouldn't stop shaking. I felt compelled to rip up the garbage I had just written.

The deadline for my writing assignment was looming. With only a few days remaining I had an assignment to write a 3,000 word piece. The main character in my fictional story was to be a teenage boy who struggled to come to grips with his imminent death.

I searched the net for Munch's painting 'The Scream' to provide a visual image that might help me to illustrate real-life agony. This God-awful picture succeeded only in making me depressed and frightened. I couldn't find the perfect adjectives, nouns or verbs to show such deep hurt.

My concentration was out of focus until an idea came to me. If I could force myself to recall that horrible mayday dream I had years before of Don in distress on his boat I might be able to weave the nightmarish pictures into a poignant story. Don's frightful image would probably be a bit cloudy after ten years, but I decided to give it a try.

The nightmare came back to me, but this time it was somehow more intense, more disturbing. As Don was fighting for his life he sent out a mayday plea for help from the helm of his boat.

MAY DAY. MAY DAY. MAY DAY.

Don's misshapen face was nothing like the handsome man we all knew and loved. His engaging smile was gone; his love of excitement absent and his self-assured confidence was missing. Rose wasn't at his side. He was alone and lost in the storm of his life.

At that moment I was panic stricken and knew I had to give up on this disturbing image and write about something with a happier ending.   Within minutes a certain calm and sense of well-being replaced my fears and I knew I would be able to sleep in peace now that the fictitious scenario was laid to rest.

The next afternoon as Glenn I were sitting in our living room chatting with friends we started to talk about Don and Rose's holiday.

"Sure hope Don and Rose are having fun in Victoria and Don is feeling okay after his scare last week."

"He'll be fine," Frank replied. "The doctor gave him a clean bill of health, and besides he loves any excuse to spend time on his new pride and joy 'Eco' even when it's docked."

"Yeah, you're right. He's probably sitting at the helm with his ball cap turned backwards wearing one of his favourite wool sweaters, sipping on a cup of black coffee."

"I bet Rose and their daughter Nancy are off shopping like mad," speculated Marie.

I jumped up to answer the phone on the third ring when I saw Don's daughter Jennifer's name on the call display.

"Hi, Jen. How's it going? Hear anything from your long-lost parents?"

From her flat, somber voice it was obvious something was dramatically wrong.

"I hate to tell you this on the phone. My dad died yesterday. He was alone on his boat when he had a massive heart attack."

Did I have a premonition last night or was Don really trying to get in touch with me? Were all signals now cut off forever? No more mayday calls, no more mind games, no more fun? We wouldn't be able to hear Don's voice saying with his wry grin, "I just dodged another bullet."

Communications were suspended on September 22nd 2006. But in my heart I knew we would always keep in touch.

And it wasn't over yet.

January 22nd 2007.

This New Zealand holiday wasn't the same without Don and Rose. The four of us loved the Bay of Plenty area where we had stayed every year beginning in 2001. Hundreds of photos show our joy walking on the beach, and happy times with our lifetime friends. It was truly Godzone.

On Saturday morning we followed our old tradition that we had with the Grants. Glenn cooked pancakes on the outdoor grill and attempted to make scrambled eggs the way Don loved them. I gave a toast to our buddies and thanked them in absentia for their friendship that dated back to the early 70s.

Still in a nostalgic mood we drove towards the Mount on Marine Parade turning left on Banks Ave. toward Pilot Bay. As we reached the top of the small hill we spotted a towering cruise ship at the wharf.

"If Don were here he'd be snapping pictures like crazy. He sure loved those cruise ships"

As Glenn turned to the right onto Shadelands Lane we saw a huge For Sale billboard on the corner. The giant words stared right at us.

MAYDAY.

MAYDAY.

"Look at that sign. Don must be here!"

"Calm down, Nancy, if Don were here it would have to be a Re-Max sign. You know that."

No sooner had he uttered these words when in disbelief we noticed the car driving past us in the opposite direction had a red, white and blue Re-Max sign painted on the door.

Okay, Don. You won this time.

Fake It

As I finger the hand-painted worry stone hidden in the side pocket of my skirt the inscription *Fake It* reminds me that I must keep the faith and pretend I'm successful and happy. Every day I repeat slogans memorized from countless real estate seminars.

Think only positive thoughts about yourself and others.

You're successful and people love you.

When the going gets tough, the tough get going.

This afternoon, like any other afternoon, I sit at my fake walnut desk in my drab bull-pen office. I detest this room. It's bare and humdrum like a school classroom with its plain and functional furniture. Walls stained yellow with cigarette smoke cry despair to me and my fellow realtors.

I steadfastly practise writing phony 'offers to purchase' as the hours crawl by. John Dough is my fictitious buyer and Isabelle Heartbroken is the seller.

Am I fooling anyone?

I kid myself into believing my fake deals will keep me in good form and prepared. 1975 has been a tough year for me. It's been six months since my last sale.

My insane practice goes on until I'm the lone realtor left in the office. It's my duty day, which means I'm entitled to all walk-in customers. But not one person has crossed the threshold.

I'm lucky I don't need to worry about getting a sitter for the kids since my husband Mark is now unemployed. Usually I'm late, but today I promised I would get home in time for a family dinner. I toss the ripped-up shreds of paper into the waste paper bin and wander over to the plate glass window to survey the near-empty main street of downtown Kelowna.

It's deserted except for a tall, twenty-something guy checking out our display window. He's wearing a black long-sleeved shirt, bola tie, Stetson hat and tight jeans. This stylish dude could have stepped off a Hollywood set. He's hot in a cool, sexy way.

I bet he thinks the faded pictures of stale-on-the-market homes are totally lackluster and boring. Nothing catches his attention except the photos of the sales staff. He smiles as he looks straight at me.

I blush. He must have seen my photo. The 10x12 glossy is displayed along with those of four other women and ten male salesmen. Most look like a police line-up. Mine is different. My Afro hair-style and dangling earrings are frivolous in contrast to the old lady hairspray-jobs of my female colleagues. I'm a career woman, but not the stuffy kind.

I step out onto the scorching sidewalk.

"Can I help you, sir?"

He turns, gives me another big grin as he tips his hat.

"Well, ma'am, I sure hope so."

This remark, subtly suggestive, unexpectedly thrills me. His black ten gallon hat, tilted forward, creates a mysterious element to his macho good looks. He scans me up and down. I've almost forgotten what it's like to have a real man flirt with me.

"No need to call me ma'am. Patricia Caliente is my name, but if you prefer, you can call me Pat. Come inside and tell me what you're looking for."

"Delighted to, ma'am."

He pulls two chairs together as he continues his staring game.

"Dave Fox is my name, and I hail from Calgary. I travel with the Canadian Rodeo Tour and I'm on the hunt for a ranch, about 100 acres or so, with irrigation water. We have over fifty head of horses and will need about two acres per head."

I'm barely listening.

Is he married? Is he rich? He did say we? Probably not a good sign.

"About how much can you spend for the right piece, Dave?"

He rubs his nose.

"Price doesn't matter if the piece suits my needs."

"By the way, Dave, I didn't get your number."

"It's okay, I've got yours."

I don't have a clue about horses, rodeos, or bare land, but I can play the role and put on a good show.

Anything to make a sale. Anything for a little adventure.

"There aren't many properties with irrigation water in this area. We'll have to drive out to the South Okanagan to look around."

He yawns.

"Don't sweat it, sweetheart. I'm a slow, easy kind of guy and I'm more than willing to spend time with you getting to know the lay of the land."

"Let's meet back here tomorrow morning, Dave, and spend the day together. Would ten o'clock suit you?"

"Okay, Pat. I'll be waiting."

He leaves. I lock the office and race down the block to my clunker '67 Chevy. In my excitement I forget to buckle up. I get home in record time after running every caution light along the way.

Mark has made vegetarian chili using all the leftovers in the fridge. He's a pretty good cook and makes some delicious meals out of nothing, but like most of his dishes, this chili lacks spice. I explain almost everything to Mark about my new client's requirements.

"Can you think of a good property?"

Instead of a helpful answer I get, as usual, a negative rant.

"You can't go off with a perfect stranger to look at properties in some godforsaken area."

His eggshell ego is starting to crack. Does he realize I'm a little too eager? Too bad he doesn't have a job or any prospects of one.

I spend the evening analyzing the catalogue of MLS listings. By midnight, I've narrowed the choices down to a couple of properties located south of Kelowna between Osoyoos and Rock Creek.

Now I must get some beauty sleep to be at my best tomorrow. Mark is snoring when I slip into the far side of our king-size waterbed. My brain is buzzing with images of every item in my closet jumping in and out of focus.

What should I wear? My see-through blouse and white pants might be too suggestive. The last time I wore that outfit I was ten pounds lighter and five years younger. My black shirt-waist dress was appropriate for Dad's funeral, but lacks any sex appeal. It bugs the hell out of me that Mark can fall asleep every single night within five seconds of hitting the pillow.

When the sun suddenly shines through the window I finally make my decision. A pure-white blouse with a black mini-skirt that shows off my shapely legs will do the trick. I will leave the worry stone behind.

I arrive ten minutes early. Tex is waiting, slouched against the building smoking a Marlborough, wearing the same get-up as yesterday minus the tie.

"Good morning Dave. I'm all set to go, but would you mind driving your car? My air conditioning is on the blink and today will be a scorcher."

"I'd love to, but my new Cadillac isn't being delivered to the dealer for a few days. I flew into town from Calgary. Don't worry. I love the heat - the hotter the better. I'll drive your car and you can sit back and enjoy the ride."

This idea appeals to me.

I want to slack-off for a day. Give over all control. Leave irksome obligations at home.

Dave's driving is reckless. I don't give a damn. The wind in my face feels good and I relish a reprieve from the constant demands of my husband, kids and high-maintenance clients.

Dave expounds on his expertise at bareback riding and tie-down roping. He bores me to death with a detailed report of his wild, carefree life with the rodeo, and the countless groupies who are attracted to him.

"I have to fight off these aggressive, wild women. They're all over me. I'm single and do like a variety of one night stands. But now Í want a real woman, someone who knows how to deliver."

I keep my mouth shut, but inside I cringe.

Two hours down the road Dave suggests a lunch break when he spots a cheap diner on the highway past the town of Osoyoos. Dave takes the lead and steers me to a booth in the back corner. We squeeze tight together. His sweaty hand is hot on my knee while I sit frozen to the fake leather seat.

My eyes fixate on the half-empty salt and pepper shakers in the centre of the table as his stare pierces clear through to my core. Without warning erect nipples protrude through the thin polyester of my damp blouse. Dave smirks as his hand travels over my nylons to the top of my thigh.

Probably most women he knows don't wear anything under their skirts.

His fingers stop roaming when the ageing waitress saunters over. Her knowing look is filled with contempt as she takes our order. I'm queasy so I opt for toast and hot tea. After his main course Dave orders apple pie with ice cream.

How could he eat a heavy dessert after he just devoured roast beef with Yorkshire pudding along with a jug of draft beer?

"I would have paid the bill, darling, but I forgot my wallet and this cafe only takes cash. Would you mind?"

With one hand on the wheel I can only guess what's on his mind. Heat waves rise above the dry, dusty expanse. After an hour we arrive at the first acreage. Dave isn't impressed.

"Nope, it's too small for my needs".

He pulls over long enough to relieve himself beside the car. No hand washing for this cowboy. I'm preoccupied with worries about his next daring move, but try to let it go and concentrate on the job at hand.

By now I'm beginning to wonder, with my usual bad luck, if he's a rapist or a serial killer on the loose.

The next showing is eighty kilometers away. I keep my distance, sit close to the window and hug the door. Half-way there he spots a pub and decides to stop for another beer. A broken-down sign hangs on a rusty hook. It reads 'Last Stop Sucker.' Probably another bad omen.

Dave loves the western décor and looks right at home with two beers and crispy fries. I agree to have a beer if it's in a tall, frosty glass. Dave strolls over to check out an ancient jukebox stuck in the middle of the dance floor, sticky with remnants of spilled drinks. Patsy Cline's hit *Crazy* fills the bar.

"Patsy, this is my favorite song. May I have this dance?"

I hate to be called Patsy.

He presses his hard body firmly against me and whispers in my ear.

"You're like an untamed filly about to be broken. You're one hot babe."

His scent, musk, coupled with the beer on his breath is dangerously exciting.

Now I'm scared of my own cravings. What would Mark think if he found me dancing with a cowboy in the middle of the afternoon?

It's my fault our marriage has dried out, but after a ton of unsatisfied longings I need some breathing room.

After another dance to 'I Fall to Pieces' I again pay the bill and we leave in silence.

When we finally find the property in Bridesville, it has to be a hundred degrees in the shade. No sliver of relief is offered by the spindly lodge-pole pines peppering the rolling hills. We trudge on foot up and down, over and over, one ridge after another. I should have chosen cool cotton instead of polyester.

My high heel shoes are no match for Dave's snakeskin boots. Thistle burrs stick to my nylons. I feel like Dave is stalking me from behind. Without a hat or water I could have heatstroke.

Why the hell didn't I dress for this sauna-heat of the desert? I hate myself for being such a show-off.

With so much territory left to view Dave suggests I remove my nylons and get comfortable before we drive over the remaining hundred acres.

Like myself, my car can't handle washboard gravel trails and extreme heat. It bounces and shudders, until we hear a loud clunk. Dave inspects the damage and reports with authority that the tail pipe has broken off from the muffler.

Great, now I'm stuck in the middle of Canada's Sonoran Desert with Billy the Kid!

Being a pro Dave is in his element. He hums 'Home on the Range' as he uses a rope from the trunk to tie the tail pipe to the frame. It works and is secure enough to hold for awhile. To celebrate his feat Dave asks if I want to smoke some weed.

"Smoke some weed! What do you mean?"

He laughs and gives me a big bear-hug. The cigarette smells sweet and foreign.

It must be a new brand. I might as well have one although I haven't had a puff since high school; then I'll manoeuver the conversation to closing the sale.

I rattle on and on about the great possibilities of this last parcel. I lie and tell Dave he could make a lot of money in the future. His horses would love the open terrain, not to mention that it's common knowledge women are attracted to a man with a big spread.

Dave interrupts my sales pitch before I have time to finish my smoke

"Let's go back to Kelowna and try again tomorrow."

"Sorry, Dave, I'm tied up tomorrow and all week. But this is a good property and I think you better put in an offer before someone else does. When would you like possession?"

"I reckon whatever dates suit the owner would be okay, but hey! I want some time to think about it. I hate like hell being rushed, so just back off, bitch."

I'm crushed. I hate Mr Dave Fox and all buyers in general, but I'm not going to let this cowboy off the hook.

"Could it be the money, Dave?"

"Of course not, but I need some time to confirm matters with my financial advisors"

I've heard this bull before.

Back in the car I try to keep my cool even though I'm at the end of my rope. Dave starts to tell me more stories. That's when I cut him off at the pass by pleading I'm too tired for chatter. I pretend I'm asleep.

Dave pipes up with yet another great idea.

"Let's stop for pizza before we go back to the office."

"Look, I'm sorry, but you'll have to eat by yourself."

"Ah, Patsy, don't be like that. You know I just want to spend more time with you."

"So long, Dave. It's been a slice, but I just want to go home."

At last I'm back in Kelowna with my life and my underwear still intact. As I get through the door Mark wants to hear all about my day.

"I'm too tired to talk now. I want to go to bed. See you in the morning."

On Sunday I sleep in and try to forget my Wild West hangover. Mark has sense enough not to question me.

Monday's a new beginning although I can't stop doing instant replays of the fiasco with my rodeo guy. In the coffee room at the office I hear the secretary call me to the front.

There's Tex dressed in his now familiar costume. He reeks of a blend of beer and B.O. I could be imagining things, but I think I can detect a trace of that strange cigarette smoke. He's carrying a weakly cactus plant.

"Hi, Patsy, I want to thank you for all your time and trouble and hope you will forgive my crude behavior. I know you're a real lady. I just got carried away with your good looks. Here's a little peace offering for you. I've spoken to my lawyer and financial advisor and they told me to go ahead and make an offer on the Bridesville ranch."

YES! St. Jude the patron saint of the hopeless has performed a miracle.

"That's great news, Dave. You're making the right choice. Have a seat and I'll get you a coffee."

I'm too cynical. Dave's truly a good guy.

I prepare the detailed offer and Dave scribbles his name at the bottom of the contract. As I parade down the aisle to show my manager the paper-work, I do a quick calculation and figure I'll make around three grand. That'll be enough to pull us out of arrears on our mortgage payments. But I mustn't get ahead of myself.

Mr Bolton suggests I ask Dave to have his cheque certified before I present the offer to the owners.

The Bank of Montreal is only three blocks down the street. Dave says he'll be right back with the cheque. When I call Mark with the news he sounds like the guy I married, positive and proud. He suggests we get a babysitter and go out for dinner and a movie to celebrate my success.

It shouldn't take over an hour even if Dave has stopped for something to eat. I stroke my worry stone until my fingers threaten to go into spasm and tell myself to calm down and relax.

There's a one hour time difference in Calgary. Maybe that could be the reason for the delay. Perhaps the manager wasn't available.

Soon my uncontrolled joy changes to tears as I leave the office.

The following morning I get a call.

"Hi, Patsy, this is Dave. I'm sorry I didn't come back yesterday, but believe it or not I'm in the slammer. The cops arrested me on a couple of trumped-up charges that won't stick. I know this is asking a lot, but is there any chance you could put up bail?

"Bail? You've got to be joking."

"I wouldn't ask, but I'm in a terrible bind and I can't reach my fuckin' lawyer. I really need your help. You and I could make it big if we were a team."

"Stop calling me Patsy! And the answer is NO."

I slam down the phone and resolve never to speak to the creep again.

The next day my manager calls out to me.

"Hey, Pat, isn't this your rodeo guy?"

There's no mistaking it. There's Dave's picture on the third page of the *Daily Courier* with the caption, COWBOY LASSOED IN KELOWNA. It goes on to say that Ralph Cooper, alias Dave Fox, was arrested on Bernard Avenue and charged with possession of illegal drugs. He's being held at the city jail pending trial in Calgary on outstanding Canada-wide warrants for sexual assault, fraud, cultivation and distribution of marijuana. The trial will be held in Calgary in six weeks. .

Six months later I still feel like a has-been hooker hoping to make a fast buck on my last trick of the night. Shards of broken dreams stick in my mind as I search for clues to my now withered marriage. It's tough to repair a failing relationship.

While reading Eric Berne's book *Games People Play* I glance at the deformed cactus plant and fantasize how my life could have been with someone like Dave.

I wish I could find a man with Mark's steadiness, and Dave's sex appeal...

January is a good time to conjure up new goals and throw away all negative thoughts. The past year is behind me and almost forgotten, when a male voice on the phone asks to speak to Mrs Caliente.

"This is Pat Caliente speaking. How may I help you?"

"I'd like to have some information on the Fixer-Upper advertised in today's paper. The one that says it's vacant and available for quick possession."

"Yes, sir, that's a real bargain. It won't stick around for long. You'll have to act fast on this one. I'd be happy to show you the property. When can we get together?"

"Hey, Patsy darling, don't you recognize my voice? It's me, Dave. Your favourite cowboy. I got off on a technicality and I'm ready to ride.

"Are you available this afternoon?"

"Maybe."

Take it Easy

Blanche's nerves are shot. She needs to get back her life and start having some fun. After all, she's just 65-years old, still attractive and everyone tells her she's a smart dresser.

As she glances out the window of the bus she doesn't notice the traffic whizzing by or hear the roar of motorcycles and cars. Instead she concentrates on her inner voice telling her to take charge. She gets off the bus in front of the mall and walks toward an aging white Ford Focus with the words Easy Drive Lessons painted in bright orange on the side panel of the door.

Blanche flinches at the sight of the driving instructor leaning against the car smoking a cigarette; his beer-belly overhanging his baggy jeans.

"Hi, I'm Harold, and you must be Blanche."

"I'm so pleased to meet you, Harold."

"Me, too. But how'd you hear about me?"

"You taught my girlfriend Stella Stringer some years ago."

"Oh, yeah. I remember her. Is the old gal still in that old folk's home? Still Waters, wasn't it? How's she doin'?"

"Yes she is still there, and she is just fine. Thanks for asking. Do you think you can really teach me to drive again?"

"Of course, honey. I've been drivin' forever. I started this game when I quit driving a bus."

"You're still quite young. May I ask why you quit?"

"I was a nervous wreck. Snot-nose kids were gettin' to me. I got so I couldn't take the little buggers."

"I know what you mean. Children today haven't any proper manners."

"Besides the old ticker was giving me problems so I figured it was best to quit while I was ahead. So, sweetheart, have you ever driven a car before?"

"Yes, quite a lot when I was a teenager, but that changed when I got married. Harry never trusted me behind the wheel. He only allowed me to drive once in a while so I turned in my license shortly after he died."

"That's a shame. Some guys just hate lady drivers. You can trust me. I guarantee you'll soon be peeling rubber."

"I'm still a bit edgy. Harry passed away a year ago, but I still have awful nightmares about his death. It's even hard to look at our beloved Jaguar parked in the garage."

"A Jag? Wow! How cool is that? He must have left you a few bucks, eh? How'd he die anyway?"

"If you don't mind, Harold, I'd rather not get into it right now. At the present time I just want to get my confidence back."

"Okey-dokey, but before we start here's the deal. Three lessons for a hundred bucks cash, and no receipts"

"All right, but I'll have to bring the money tomorrow. I only have my credit card with me today. To be honest, Harold, I'm disappointed that I can't collect any travel points."

"Live with it, honey. I'm giving you one hell of a deal."

"Sorry. I just thought it wouldn't hurt to ask."

"Whatever. Now let's get started. You can get behind the wheel and buckle up. Check the rear-view and side-view mirrors. Tell yourself you're calm and in perfect control."

"Don't worry. I'm always under control and I'm a fast learner."

"Okay. Put it in drive and we'll see how you do."

Blanche adjusts the mirrors and powders her nose before putting the car in gear. Next time she will remember to bring some aerosol spray to get rid of the disgusting smell of tobacco and grease that permeates his vehicle. She pulls away quickly as she rolls the window down.

"See, there's nothing to it. Cruise along and enjoy the ride. Now slow down. There's a car pulling out just ahead. Slow down. Slow down, Blanche! For God's sake, take it easy."

With a nervous smile Blanche says, "I think I'll hit that car."

"Use the fuckin' brake!"

"I can't my heel is caught in your carpet."

Harold slams his foot on the brake, nearly crushing her foot. The car comes to an abrupt stop.

"Harold, I would appreciate it if you would watch your language. I'm a Christian woman and besides you sounded just like my husband."

"Well you damned near killed us. I'm sure the Lord would understand. So that's it for today, Blanche. I'll take over now."

"This lesson had better be complimentary. I only got to drive for five minutes and I was just starting to have a good time."

"That's too bad, but I've had enough. See ya tomorrow."

"Goodbye, Harold, and sorry for the little scare, but I'm on anti-depressants, and not my usual self. By the way would you mind dropping me off at the grocery store? The one at the mall gives points, unlike some companies I know."

Harold shakes his head and gives her a salute while she gets in the passenger side. His gut tells him she's going to be a royal pain in the ass, but he decides to suck it up and try his best to make a few bucks.

The next day Blanche knocks on his window and motions to Harold to get on the other side.

"Hello, Harold. Did you manage to sleep well last night?"

"Yeah, I'm fine. I took a Valium along with my blood pressure pill."

"Well, I'm feeling great and a lot more relaxed. See, I'm wearing flat shoes today."

"At least that's a step in the right direction. We'll start you off by making some right and left turns before we try parking."

"Oh, my God! I can't park. I'm too frightened to put the car in reverse."

"No sweat. Calm down. I'll show you."

"You don't understand. I don't ever want to go backwards"

"All right, forget it. Drive around the mall and always signal, even if no one is behind you. We'll practise driving into a few spots and you can try some shoulder checks. Then stop in front of McDonalds and you can buy me a coffee."

"Buy you a coffee?"

"Yes, ma'am, and don't forget the hundred bucks you owe me."

"Okay. I'll pay for the coffee, but remember nothing fancy like an iced cappuccino."

"Whatever."

Harold has met a lot of different characters in his day but Blanche is the cheapest bitch he's ever encountered. Imagine ordering two senior coffees with no mention of anything to eat with it. As he swigs down the coffee he decides to get to the bottom of her mysterious behavior.

"Hey, Blanche. Why do you have this stupid fear of backing up?"

"It's a long story. I'll tell you tomorrow."

Harold spends a restless night on his sagging cot trying to figure out what Blanche is all about. He fantasizes that she's filthy rich, and not having any relatives leaves him a huge inheritance.

Blanche can't sleep either. She's too giddy with excitement for tomorrow's lesson.

"Good morning, Harold. Isn't it a great day for a relaxing drive?"

As Blanche gets behind the wheel she inquires why he has the engine running.

"The battery is a bit low so that'll help charge it up. But before we begin, tell me why you're so damn nervous?"

"Well, it's upsetting, but my therapist tells me it's good to talk about it."

"Spit it out, sweetheart."

"Harry didn't suffer long. It was sudden and such a shock. I didn't see him taking out the garbage when I backed right into him. He died within minutes so it wasn't too bad"

"No kidding. Blanche, do you mean you actually ran over him? Holy shit."

"The police knew it was an accident, but somehow I got a thrill out of it. I loved the adrenalin rush and I took to running over anything that was near my car, like neighbourhood cats and the occasional dog."

"Didn't anyone blow the whistle on you?"

"Yes. Some mean-spirited busybody called the authorities. I can't believe some people are so crazy about their pets."

"Did they lock you up?"

"No. But they demanded that I stop driving for six months, take psychotherapy and enrol in driver training. My probation is over now, and I'm itching to get back behind the wheel. Your training will help me get my license back."

"Blanche, that is fucking sick! You must be nuts. Lady you do need help, but not from me. Now get the hell out of my car and don't expect a refund either."

Harold reckons he'll have to forego his inheritance.

"Calm down, Harry - I mean Harold. I understand how you feel. Maybe I'm not ready to start driving again. I promise I won't bother you again."

As Harold moves to get out of the car he says, "Don't turn off the engine Blanche. I'll come around to get in."

Blanche smiles as she puts the car in reverse. The car lurches backward with a heavy thud.

Blanche turns off the ignition and touches up her lipstick in the mirror before she struts back to the bus stop. The fresh air makes her feel intoxicated and proud of herself.

She's confident that she did Harold a big favour and prays that he enjoys eternal peace.

As she rides home on the crowded bus she begins to relish the thought of searching for a new instructor. *Preferably a handsome Christian man with good manners, a gentleman with class. Someone who appreciates a real lady.*

About the Author

Nancy was born in 1941, the last of five siblings, and raised in the inner city of Windsor, Ontario. Educated by nuns at Catholic schools she graduated from Grade 13 and then attended teacher's college in London, Ontario.

She married Glenn Crouchman, her high school boyfriend, shortly after she turned 20. Her brief and intermittent teaching career was interrupted by the birth of three daughters between 1962 and 1965.

In 1968 Nancy embarked on a new career in real estate, again interrupted in 1970 by the birth of another daughter.

Glenn's transfer to Kelowna, British Columbia, in 1973 meant relocating the family and finding new friends and interests. There Nancy started a book club that is still going strong.

A return to her real estate career accompanied by Glenn provided a more stable, albeit still stressful family life. As owners of their own real estate office they retired in 2000 and began their annual winter escapes to the wonderfully warm New Zealand summers.

With a lingering childhood desire to write Nancy joined a number of writing groups in Kelowna as well as Tauranga Writers in New Zealand.

On her return to Canada she began courses in creative writing through the University of British Columbia and Okanagan College.

A number of her pieces have been included in *Papershell*, the University's annual creative writing anthology, and *Breeze* magazine in New Zealand.